FRENCH
VOICES

FRENCH
VOICES

Winner of the French Voices Award

www.frenchbooknews.com

IN THE UNITED STATES OF AFRICA

ABDOURAHMAN A. WABERI

Translated by David and Nicole Ball
Foreword by Percival Everett

University of Nebraska Press ▪ Lincoln

This work, published as part of a program providing publication assistance, received financial support from the French Ministry of Foreign Affairs, the Cultural Services of the French Embassy in the United States and FACE (French American Cultural Exchange).

Cet ouvrage, publié dans le cadre d'un programme d'aide à la publication, bénéficie du soutien financier du ministère des Affaires étrangères, du Service culturel de l'ambassade de France aux États-Unis, ainsi que de l'appui de FACE (French American Cultural Exchange).

Library of Congress Cataloging-in-Publication Data

Waberi, Abdourahman A., 1965–
[Aux États-Unis d'Afrique. English]
In the United States of Africa / Abdourahman
A. Waberi ; translated by David and Nicole Ball ;
foreword by Percival Everett.
p. cm.
ISBN 978-0-8032-1391-3 (cloth : alk. paper) —
ISBN 978-0-8032-2262-5 (pbk. : alk. paper)
I. Ball, David, 1937– II. Ball, Nicole, 1941–
III. Title.
PQ2683.A23A9813 2009
843'.914—dc22   2008027597

Set in Scala by Bob Reitz.
Designed by Ashley Muehlbauer.

To the memory of François-Xavier Verschave,
for his courage and commitment.

For my translators: Jeanne Garane,
Marie-José Hoyet, and Dominic Thomas,
most gratefully.

And, of course, to
David and Nicole Ball.

FOREWORD

I was flattered when offered the opportunity to write this preface for Abdourahman Waberi's *Aux États-Unis d'Afrique*. Then I became nervous, and as happens with most of us, my nervousness turned to outright panic in the face of the actual pages. Then I recalled my one meeting with Abdourahman, in St. Malo on the French coast. He was with his young son. I was taken with both of them and what they shared, an intense gaze and a readiness to laugh. I expected and found these traits in this novel, in English, *In the United States of Africa*, and then my panic turned to excitement.

I am happy for Abdourahman that his novel has found not only fine translators, David and Nicole Ball, but a very fine and solid publisher, the University of Nebraska Press. It's a shame that in this country we consider it daring when a house chooses to publish translations of fiction by writers other than the really well known names. British publishers are far better at it than we. European houses translate and publish other languages energetically and to the eager anticipation of their readers. We, perhaps out of xenophobic reflex or, more likely, mere laziness, show little interest in the art of the rest of the world. And so we should applaud the efforts of the few presses in the United States that take it upon themselves to widen our reading and therefore our understanding of other nations and cultures.

The planet rotates on its axis. Gravity works in but one direction and everything spins one way, tilting and celestially observed retrograde motion notwithstanding. And yet when I buy a globe, Europe is on top and Africa is on the bottom. When photos come back from the space shuttle, the picture is oriented the same, as if there is a top and a bottom in space. Even if I invert my globe, as it will allow, the words, the names of places and geologic sites are now upside down. The world makes no sense with the South Pole on the top.

This is where *In the United States of Africa* enters the picture. Abdourahman Waberi has inverted the globe and has managed as well to turn over the writing. By this act of inversion he has allowed us to see the absurdity of any kind of oriented globe. This novel holds a mirror up to the planet and questions the direction of spin, whether gravity is a pulling or pushing force, whether upside-down writing is even writing at all.

This novel does more than pose pedestrian counterfactual representations of the global standard state of affairs. It takes our accepted pictures of the world and inverts them, much as a mathematician or geometrician might proceed with a proof by negating what is perceived to be true. And the book does so with such apparent ease.

This is a novel of ideas. The stories and characters do not traverse the usual, predictable trails. It is a refreshingly impressionistic work. Sounds are laid beside each other, as are images, as are ideas, notions, fabrications, misapprehensions. It is in many ways wildly French, the attention to sentences, the haunting almost musical phrasing, as in Debussy or Saint-Saëns, but it is also straight from the heart of Djibouti, intensely intellectual and polyphonic.

I congratulate the University of Nebraska Press for demonstrating the kind of love of and devotion to literature that we need more of in this country. I congratulate David and Nicole Ball for their fine translation. And I of course congratulate Abdourahman Waberi for writing a novel I wish I could have written.

Percival Everett
Los Angeles CA
December 1, 2007

IN THE UNITED STATES OF AFRICA

ONE
A Voyage to Asmara, the Federal Capital

1 *In which the author gives a brief account of the origins of our prosperity and the reasons why the Caucasians were thrown onto the paths of exile.*

He's there, exhausted. Silent. The wavering glow of a candle barely lights the carpenter's bedroom in this shelter for immigrant workers. This ethnically Swiss Caucasian speaks a Germanic dialect, and in this age of the jet and the Internet, claims he has fled violence and famine. Yet he still has all of the aura that fascinated our nurses and aid workers.

Let's call him Yacuba, first to protect his identity and second because he has an impossible family name. He was born outside Zurich in an unhealthy favela, where infant mortality and the rate of infection by the AIDS virus remain the highest in the world today. The figures are drawn from studies of the World Health Organization (WHO) based in our country in the fine, peaceful city of Banjul, as everyone knows. AIDS first appeared in Greece some two decades ago in the shady underworld of prostitution, drugs, and promiscuity and is now endemic worldwide, according to the high priests of world science at the Mascate meeting in the noble kingdom of Oman.

The cream of international diplomacy also meets in Banjul; they are supposedly settling the fate of millions of Caucasian refugees of various ethnic groups (Austrian, Canadian, American, Norwegian, Belgian, Bulgarian, Hungarian, British, Icelandic, Swedish, Portuguese . . .) not to mention the skeletal boat people from the northern Mediterranean, at the end of their rope from dodging all the mortar shells and missiles that darken the unfortunate lands of Euramerica.

Some of them cut and run, wander around, get exhausted, and then brusquely give up, until they are sucked into the void. Prostitutes of every sex, Monte Carlians or Vaticanians but others too, wash up on the Djerba beaches and the cobalt-blue bay of Algiers. These poor devils are looking for the bread, rice, or flour distributed by Afghan, Haitian, Laotian, or Sahelian aid organizations. Ever since our world has been what it is, little French, Spanish, Batavian, or Luxembourgian schoolchildren, hit hard by kwashiorkor, leprosy, glaucoma, and poliomyelitis, survive only with food surpluses from Vietnamese, North Korean, or Ethiopian farmers.

These warlike tribes with their barbaric customs and deceitful, uncontrollable moves keep raiding the scorched lands of the Auvergne, Tuscany or Flanders, when they're not shedding the blood of their atavistic enemies—Teutons, Gascons, or backward Iberians—for the slightest little thing, for rifles or trifles, because they recognize a prisoner or because they don't. They're all waiting for a peace that has yet to come.

But let us return to the shack of our flea-ridden Germanic or Alemanic carpenter. Take a furtive look into the darkness of his dwelling. A mud floor scantily strewn with wood shavings, no furniture or utensils. No electricity or running water, of course. This individual, poor as Job on his dung heap, has never seen a trace of soap, cannot imagine the flavor of yogurt, has no conception of the sweetness of a fruit salad. He is a thousand miles from our most basic Sahelian conveniences. Which is further from us, the moon, polished by Malian and Liberian astronauts, or this creature?

Let us cross what we might call the threshold: swarms of flies block your view and a sour smell immediately grabs you by the throat. You try to move forward nonetheless, but you can't. You stand there, dumbstruck.

Your eyes are beginning to get used to the darkness. You can make out the contours of what seems to be a painting with crude patterns. One of those daubs called primitive: clueless tourists are crazy about them. Two crossed zebu horns and a Protestant sword decorate the other side of the wall, a sign of the religious zeal that pervades this shelter for foreign workers in our rich, dynamic Eritrean state.

Let us say in passing that our values of solidarity, conviviality, and morality are now threatened by rapid social transformations and the violent unleashing of the unbridled free market, as the Afrigeltcard has replaced our ancestral traditions of mutual aid. The ancient country of Eritrea, governed for centuries by a long line of Muslim puritans, deeply influenced by the rigorism of the Senegalese Mourides, was able to prosper by combining good business sense with the virtues of parliamentary democracy. From its business center in Massawa or its online stock market on Lumumba Street, not to mention the very *high-tech Keren Valley Project*[1] and the military-industrial complexes in Assab, everything here works together for success and prosperity. This is what attracts the hundreds of thousands of wretched Euramericans subjected to a host of calamities and a deprivation of hope.

Our carpenter is muttering in his beard. What can he possibly be saying with his tongue rolled up at the back of his throat? God alone could decipher his white pidgin dialect. He is racked by the desire to leave the cotton fields of his slavery—quite understandable, but let's get back to the subject.

Still more dizzying is the flow of capital between Eritrea and its dynamic neighbors, who are all members of the federation of the United States of Africa, as is the former Hamitic kingdom of Chad, rich in oil; and also the ex-Sultanate of Djibouti that handles millions of guineas and surfs on its gas boom; or the Madagascar archipelago, birthplace of the conquest of space and tourism for the enfants terribles of the new high finance. The golden boys of Tananarive are light-years away from the black wretchedness of the white Helvetian carpenter.

You're still standing? Ah, okay! Now you recognize a familiar sound. You try a risky maneuver, taking one, then two steps into the darkness. You walk through the tiny door. You can make out the first measures of some mumbo jumbo full of shouts and strangled sounds. An antediluvian black and white TV, made in Albania, dominates the living room of this shelter for destitute Caucasians, with their straight hair and infected lungs. After an insipid soap opera, a professor from the

1. In English in the original.—Translators' note.

Kenyatta School of European and American Studies,[2] an eminent special-
ist in Africanization—the latest fad in our universities, now setting
the tone for the whole planet—claims that the United States of Africa
can no longer accommodate all the world's poor. You might be taken
in by his unctuous voice as you listen to him, but in fact his polished
statements, all cheap lace and silk rhetoric, fool nobody—certainly
not the immigrants from outside Africa. His idea can be summed
up in one sentence: the federal authorities must face up to their re-
sponsibilities firmly but humanely by escorting all foreign nationals
back to the border, by force if necessary—first the illegal immigrants,
then the semi-legal, then the paralegal, and so on.

Alternative voices have arisen, all or almost all from liberal circles
which hardly needed the TV talks of Professor Emeritus Garba Hunt-
ingwabe to react against "the irrational fear of the Other, of 'undesir-
able aliens,' that continues to be the greatest threat to African unity."
(www.foreign-policy.afr, editorial, last March.) Assembled under the
aegis of the World Academy of Gorean Cultures, which includes all
the enlightened minds in the world from Rangoon to Lomé and from
Madras to Lusaka, these voices remind us that the millions of starving
Japanese kept alive on the food surpluses from central Africa could
be adequately taken care of with what that region spends on defense
in just three days. You may recall that the face of this network—
reviled by all the ulemas, nabobs, neguses, rais, and mwamis—is none
other than Arafat Peace Prize winner Ms. Dunya Daher of Langston
Hughes University in Harare. In September, the young ecologist put
15,800,000 guineas granted her by the austere Society of Sciences
of Botswana into the kitty of many humanitarian aid organizations.
The learned society's announcement stated that this prestigious prize
was unanimously awarded to her for "her struggle against the corrupt
dictatorship of New Zealand, her fight against AIDS [whereas] the
ecclesiastical authorities of Uganda are still preaching abstinence,
and her promotion of Nebraska bananas by vaunting their native
merits in the supermarkets of Abidjan . . . [and finally] Ms. Daher

2. In English in the original.—Translators' note.

made the world aware of the tangible facts that Dean Mamadou Diouf of the University of Gao had set forth long ago in a satirical tract that has remained famous to this day." (*Invisible Borders: The Challenge of Alaskan Immigration*, Rwanda University Press/Free Press, Kigali, 1994. 820 pp. 35 guineas.)

Dean Diouf, Ms. Daher, Ahmed Baba XV, Sophia Marley, Thomas Sankara Jr., the rappers King Cain and Queen Sheba, Hakim Bey, Siwela Nkosi and company were never in favor with the big turbans of the world. Ms. Daher deplored the silence of the political leaders of the first continent about questions crucial to the future of our planet. His Excellency El Hadj Saidou Touré, United States of Africa Press Secretary, had accustomed us to a different chant. He stated that our first priority remains keeping peace in Western Europe; and then he was relatively optimistic about signing a ceasefire in the American Midwest and Quebec, where French-speaking warlords have reiterated their firm intention of going to war with the uncontrollable English-speaking militias in the Hull region near Ottawa, the former capital, now under a curfew enforced by UN peacekeeping forces from Nigeria, Cyprus, Zimbabwe, Malawi, and Bangladesh. The federal councilor (highest political authority of what remains of Canada)—the proud aborigine William Neville Attawag—has remained extremely vague on the question of a time frame for relaxing the emergency laws now in place. Sir Attawag has violently rejected the term "apartheid" used by newspapers completely ignorant of the conditions of life for whites in the Canada of his ancestors. And yet Human Rights Watch and El Hombre, with their long experience in this North American quagmire, relentlessly keep sounding the alarm.

Yacuba has just left his shelter. He dashed into Ray Charles Avenue, caught his breath at the corner of Habib Bourguiba Street, and is now walking toward Abebe-Bikila Square. He is wearing a shirt the same color as his chronic cold; an indigo boubou floats around his body. People turn around as he walks by, more intrigued than an ethnologist taken in by a primitive tribe in the remotest parts of Bavaria. Have no fear, our long-distance cameras are recording his every move. In less than fifteen minutes, he'll be back in his den. Which won't prevent him from getting into trouble again.

Surely you are aware that our media have been digging up their most scornful, odious stereotypes again, which go back at least as far as Methusuleiman! Like, the new migrants propagate their soaring birth rate, their centuries-old soot, their lack of ambition, their ancestral machismo, their reactionary religions like Protestantism, Judaism, or Catholicism, their endemic diseases. In short, they are introducing the Third World right up the anus of the United States of Africa. The least scrupulous of our newspapers have abandoned all restraint for decades and fan the flames of fear of what has been called—hastily, to be sure—the "White Peril." Isn't form, after all, the very flesh of thought, to paraphrase the great Sahelian writer Naguib Wolegorzee? Thus, a popular daily in Ndjamena, *Bilad el Sudan*, periodically goes back to its favorite headline: "Back Across the Mediterranean, Clodhoppers!" From Tripoli, *El Ard*, owned by the magnate Hannibal Cabral, shouts "Go Johnny, Go!" Which the *Lagos Herald* echoes with an ultimatum: "White Trash, Back Home!" More laconic is the *Messager des Seychelles*, in two English words: "Apocalypse Now!"

In which we tell of an unusual young girl. A girl who will not answer the bell of her last name.

There was once a beautiful, gentle young girl. She was born with a good head. Her judgments are well founded, her heart full of goodness. She always says exactly what she thinks. She is graceful as an angel, and that's why she is called Malaïka. She grew like the grass in this land of Cockaigne, in the best of all possible families. So it was that Malaïka was first taught by her wise old father, from whom she learned to read, write, and think so quickly that soon, all by herself, she had devoured every work in the family library and many other masterpieces that are the glory of the human mind. Of all the creators who surround and enchant her, Malaïka has a weakness for the sculptors and writers of the Harlem Renaissance. Her taste for singing is beginning to grow stronger, while her venerable mother, a great lover of Somalian classical music and philology, has been, alas, struck by a mysterious illness. She has had to resign herself to the fact that she can't sing anymore and focus all her energy on other endeavors. Devastated by grief, her father, a doctor by profession, has stopped paying attention to her. From now on, Malaïka must count on herself alone.

Her real birth certificate is a veritable fairy tale. A beautiful true story. A story as delicious as a milk drink made with fresh fruits from the garden. Most of its chapters are punctuated with something bright and childish: a breath of joy that can cheer up the mournful parties of poor families, where sadness flows like mucus from the nose of the household. A tale that can make such a family forget the absent father, always wandering off or between odd jobs. Which can give fresh confidence to the mother, who holds the house together by means of federal welfare checks and various sacrifices. The life of the child who was not yet Malaïka, little Maya, flashes by in this tale. Perhaps the chaotic story of this family, told over and over in all its disorder, will give you a headache. Find your angel soul again and everything will fall into place. Can't you hear the beat of a springlike pulse rising inside you?

Wherever they may come from, children do not belong to their progenitors, their parents. They belong to themselves, that's all. They enchant our weary souls. They are born, slide along mahogany floors or roll around in the dust, grow up, leave, in turn make children who do not belong to them, and then die. Whether they sleep under slabs of Moorish marble, in Dahomeyan palaces or out in the open makes no difference. One's place of birth is only an accident; you choose your true homeland with your body and heart. You love it all your life or you leave it at once. And then, what we are going through in the present can never be seen: it is like those infrared or gamma rays that make up our environment. You are sure of this, Maya. Only later, when the blindfold of the past has been removed, do we understand it correctly. We examine the tiny shapes that time takes on. In this way, we gather the pebbles of memory to make a little pile we can decipher. This is what life teaches us if we have the wisdom to listen to it and record it, as you try to do with your clay dolls and your drawings.

Sometimes, to drain your memory, you also write and dash off sketches on rarely used supports like long bones, egg shells, or turtle shells. From your jaunts to the shores of the Red Sea or into the belly of the Sahara, you brought back a little notebook, its pages covered with your cramped, trembling handwriting. An imitation leather notebook that comes with a rubber band, the kind made famous by Aimé Césaire, Chéri Samba, Jean-Michel Basquiat, Farid Belkahia, and Kateb Yacine, according to Doctor Papa. In it, you write down your impressions, the shreds of your memories, your outbursts and outrage and the times you feel blue, just like them. At the end of your journey through words and landscapes, you come home exhausted but filled with peace beyond compare. They weren't the kind of men to pamper their phrases, caress their canvases over a brazier, or produce offspring sad as a garrison town. Their creations made their fingers stiff when they wrote or painted—that is, when they were taking the burden of destiny upon their frail shoulders. Their creations sucked their blood out. They shrunk their carcasses to the bone, to sacrifice. Left them threadbare. As for you, Malaïka, you're only beginning. But already . . . people marvel at the way you play your scales. You don't want to rot in the street like the body of a hanged man, a prey for vultures, riddled with oblivion. The end is waiting there for all of us, like the buffer at the end of the tracks. Before then, we must work, whatever the material, the mood or the season.

As a child, you were fond of walking along the ridge of the Rift hills, on the two lips of the Red Sea or in the estuary of the White Nile, following Doctor Papa on his professional peregrinations. You were trying to imagine the trip by ferry, Maya, before the Khartoum Bridge was built, well before the brand new viaduct that shortens the cross-ing, bringing you closer to the firmament and its load of stars. At the age of eight, you went all the way to the deep South on the legendary Tanzam, which connects Tanzania to Zambia, that is, the Swahili coast to Zulu country.

"Maputo! Maputo! Station stop, five minutes!" would crackle over the loudspeaker.

"Maya! Just taste this tamarind-mango juice, it's exquisite!" Doctor Papa would say.

"Watch out, Daddy, or I'll throw up in my mouth," you warned mischievously.

But you don't remember the rest because you were absorbed in the landscape going by. With your nose pressed up against the window, you hadn't budged for a second. You were only a child immersed in her daydreams. Already you were escaping far away. Like a kite, you were fluttering over the cliffs, the sand dunes, the rivers, the dark brown pebble beaches, humming what was then your favorite tune: "What is worse than a ghost? It's a bat, it's a bat!" Memories of a time gone by but drenched with so much light, with so many cries of joy.

"Come on, get out and live!" Doctor Papa would perpetually scold when he saw you in your room, lying on your belly with your head buried in a book. He used to argue that you would find nothing solid in books: one story resembles another, like grains of rice all cooked in the same way, swallowed, and forgotten just as quickly. It is highly likely, he would add, that the Sumerians invented writing not to entertain little girls of your age but for infinitely baser reasons, commercial reasons and all they entail. They perfected their fantastic invention so people could remember that this flock belonged to that clan or that crop to this family, that's all.

Ah, little Maya, Doctor Papa is very cruel, but that is the truth! We're familiar with every story since the days of Lucy, our common ancestor preserved in the anthropological museum of Addis-Ababa. So, Lucy, whose real name is Denkenech, or "little marvel" in Amharic, lies in her golden coffin, straight and proud. Yes, she truly deserved having her picture on the stamp that has just gone round the world! All stories, your father kept telling you, go through that physical and spiritual forest we call life again and again. They go around regularly like the sun. And so much the better, you would like to retort! As long as those stories haven't passed before your eyes already. Whether Doctor Papa likes it or not, as long as they haven't sifted through your brain they remain a blank slate to you. There are no new stories but there certainly are new ears for old stories like the epic of Shaka Zulu or the marvelous tales in the *Arabian Nights*, brought back from Persia and soon translated by our scholars into Malagasy, Tamasheq, Kimbundu, Sesotho, Kinyarwanda, Arabic, Aka, and Peul.

And the stories start rolling again for you alone, Maya. They take you far, as far out into the stars as the astronaut Ezra Mapanza, the first man to walk on the moon. You are still their willing captive, Maya. You drown yourself in all kinds of tales, allegories ancient or new, and every time you come out soothed, like a drowsy butterfly. And the stories roll by in high style, season after season, horizon after horizon. Ah, you don't remember where you got the image, but you are absolutely sure men are kites connected to each other by the strings of language. Sure wandering genies come out of bottles, cast a spell on crowds and extend their domination. Sure familiar voices arise and grip the heart when they don't respond to your call, confirming how close the dead really are to us. Human beings have a fleeting existence, short as the life of a bee. But the past never completely dies. The wheel of time turns. Even for you, little girl, says Doctor Papa with a wry smile, half joking, half serious. What will remain of ancient times, of the men of days gone by, beliefs that were commonplace only yesterday? Everything, and nothing. Tongues will swing into action. No respite, no rest. Myths, legends, songs, cries, and murmurs will fuse to form one single braid, a halo above our heads. A rainbow for the pleasure of the senses, and for communion. But Doctor Papa knows all that very well indeed.

3 *In which we tell of the misfortunes of the Caucasians in general and the Helvetians in particular—endless misfortunes. Yacuba puts himself in the hands of the gods. The author also tells us of an incorrigible reputation.*

Yacuba was pushed into Africa—a magical name, open Sesame!—by the militias tearing apart his postage-stamp-sized country. The clown suit called Switzerland has been subjected to ethnic and linguistic warfare for centuries and centuries. (The Belgians fare no better, but let's not go into that.) Hatreds, resentments, and dialects clash in contagious cacophony, not to mention that two-thirds of the country—snow white—is barren and uninhabitable. The north, peopled by German or Swiss German–speaking people of the Lutheran persuasion, is a bit richer than the south, a region of peasants speaking French, Italian, or Romansh, all Catholics. Hordes in various uniforms rule everywhere, devastating Helvetia. The tiny elite was the first to clear out, and every youngster's dream is to leave and go into exile. No wonder they gleefully bump each other off every three years for a dubious word, an inappropriate accent, or an occupied mountain pasture. Valaisians, Savoyards, Jurassians, Tessinians, Genevans, Lucernians, and other Schwitzers have never been able to get along. Some have their eyes and guts turned toward Germany, while the hearts of others are tuned to Paris or Milan.

Observers who came there from all over the world to try and appeal for calm and discipline yet again have learned this lesson to their cost. The slightest question asked by a foreign observer (most often United Statesian) triggers a stream of discordant responses, unearths buried resentments, and uncovers opposing strategies. You get lost in the echo of idioms at loggerheads with each other: "*Madame . . . Fräulein . . . Signorina . . .*" The linguistic borders rip apart the clown costume called Switzerland, known only for its mercenaries, its all-purpose pocket knife, and its goitered cretins. The borders divide its mountains, split its lakes, isolate villages from one another; they separate houses inside the same village and cut between the bottles sitting on the bar in the village café.

Today even more than yesterday, our African lands attract all kinds of people crushed by poverty: trollops with their feet powdered by the dust of exodus; opponents of their regimes with a ruined conscience; mangy kids with pulmonary diseases; bony, shriveled old people. People thrown into the ordeal of wandering the stony paths of exile. People facing their own filth, all cracked inside, a crown of nettles in place of a brain. You want proof, just one piece of evidence. Let us reread the centuries-old testimony of one of these poor devils, probably of the French race, who walked the twelve hundred kilometers separating Bamako from the gold-covered city: "At length, we arrived safely at Timbuktu, just as the sun was touching the horizon. I now saw this capital of the Sudan, to reach which had so long been the object of my wishes. On entering this mysterious city, which is an object of curiosity and research to all the impoverished nations of Europe, I experienced an indescribable satisfaction. I never before felt a similar emotion, and my transport was extreme" (René Caillié, 1828).[3]

You can find these same words in the toothless mouths of illegal immigrants from Porto or Odessa, Chicago or Bristol, languishing in retention centers, far from the facades, the arches, the steps and marble pediments of our cities. Nothing new under the Sahelian sun? History stammers, retracing the same steps, rushing down the same slippery slopes. Ever since Emperor Kankan Moussa, the ruler of the ancient Empire of Mali, one of the most prestigious empires of our federation, made a pilgrimage to Mecca in 1324 scattering gold along the way, all the wretched of the earth have their eyes fixed on our felicity. Now there's someone who would have gained from being as discreet and sober as our current president Nelson Mandela and his

3. *Travels through Central Africa and Across the Great Desert, to Morocco,* (London: Henry Colburn and Richard Bentley, 1830, vol. 2, p. 49), with one difference: the "impoverished nations of Europe" are "civilized nations" in Caillié.—Translators' note.

vice-president Areski Babel, both of them quite simply remarkable for their shimmering shirts, made by the designer Pathé Ndiaye himself. And thus in every elementary school textbook you find this episode that the chroniclers have trotted out a thousand times: "Emperor Kankan Moussa was at the head of a procession of sixty thousand servants and slaves to make his pilgrimage. He possessed so much gold—its weight was estimated at two to eight tons—that his visit to Cairo made the world price of gold drop fifteen to twenty percent."

And what does the chronicle (or legend?) add, intended as it is for our dear little woolly heads? "The inhabitants of Cairo were so amazed by all these mountains of gold and rivers of pearls that they broke off all ties to Constantinople, putting themselves under the protection of the son of the god-king Soundiata Keita, who also has remained in almanacs and memories for his limitless largesse. From the East, the reputation of Emperor Kankan Moussa spread at lightning speed to the farthest corners of the planet."

The Tangierian Ibn Battuta heard this legend being blown up more and more among the pagans of the Baltic islands (who practiced cannibalism) as well as the now extinct aborigines of Tasmania, and even among the quarrelsome gold diggers of Patagonia.

4 *In which we tell of the weight of the soul and various small details.*

Ever since your mother's long illness, everything—your body and your mind, your dreams and feelings—has been focused on death. You examine every sign, Maya, every word, every particle of darkness, every rumor you hear on the radio. Just yesterday, you were struck by a detail in a popular song written by our great lyric songwriter, the illustrious Robert Marley. The man who took it upon himself to caricature the whole planet and made songs out of everything. It was about the weight of the soul. They say we always lose twenty-one grams at the exact moment of our death. The scientists of Al-Azhar medical school are absolutely positive and so is the mischievous Bob. Weighing the body before and after death proves it beyond the shadow of a doubt. An ordinary healthy man is eighty percent water and twenty percent solid matter. Are those twenty-one grams really the weight of life? Of the breath? Of the soul? Of the intelligence that lifts us out of the animal kingdom? The solidity of coffins, something that usually draws us together as much from atavistic reflex as solidarity, can't do much about it. Neither can funerals and the feeling of awe that defines them. Men and women are equal in this weigh-in; male domination, perpetuated by religions, is blown into smithereens. So are prejudices, whether racial, political, or of any other kind.

You are reminded of a joke that used to be told all over the souks of Cairo, the slums of Boston and the igloos of Murmansk. A dumb joke Doctor Papa dug up in an old book of spells illustrated by Falasha monks. "I'm in love with your mother," he would whisper in your ear like a schoolboy before sharing his story with you. A woman with a passion for antiques rushes to her girlfriend to tell her she'd just bought a magic lamp. The two friends coo with pleasure. No sooner has the precious object been taken from its case scented with myrrh and aloes than the genie appears. "I would like to be the most beautiful woman in the world," says the new owner. The wish is granted on the spot. Her friend goes her one better: "I'd like to be the most beautiful—and the most intelligent." And the genie changes her into a man.

In which Caucasians, who are not people like you and me, are sent to meet their maker. The national press is in league against him, but wily Sheriff Ouedraogo doesn't let anybody step on his toes.

Melchior Ouedraogo, a little sheriff in the federal police in the state of Burkina, became famous for his expeditious treatment of the immigration issue and the overcrowding of our prisons. Every day, he throws two Caucasian bandits, two sansculottes from Prague, Trier, or Coimbra, into a ten-by-ten enclosure under a stone-breaking sun. Two men in quest of the African dream, seeking manioc and fresh water. Sheriff Ouedraogo promises to spare the life of the one who kills the other at sunset. Outcry throughout the country, the press gets involved. The churches, the rabbinate, the imamate, politicians, hoary magnates, community organizations, and even university mandarins threw in their two cents' worth.

The sheriff of the savannah braced himself on his hooves like a nervous horse. He brushed off all accusations with the back of his hand. "I'm the king on my patch of savannah," he said in his defense. "And the people here won't be afraid to support me," he added as he stormed out of his press conference. Under the stunned eyes of the reporters (who melted with envy later on), he opened the door of his office to throw himself on a huge cake covered with tapioca cream bursting with calories. An all-too-nourishing cake. He gobbled up the cake and purred with happiness before its relics dripping with shea butter. Then, totally full and quiet as a *calao*, he pointed to the way out. A week later, a press release. Grumbling, procrastination. Hiding behind the shield of the First Amendment to the Constitution. The case of *Sheriff Ouedraogo v. the State* has been postponed *sine die* by the Federal Court. Meanwhile, his ghastly idea has found receptive ears in the federal police. The Southern cattlemen, the Maghreb mounted police, the Tibesti rattlesnakes, internal security agents, the border patrol, the coast guards, the Sherpas of Kilimanjaro—everybody eagerly jumped into the hunt for immigrants. Not a day goes by without new cases of disappearances, illegal immigrants arrested and neutralized for good, illegal workers sent to meet their maker in less time than it takes to light a cigarette.

Recognizable by their uniforms and badges, these new horsemen of the apocalypse crisscross the country day and night. They wear boots, thick khaki socks halfway up their calves, and impeccably ironed shirts over sweat-absorbent T-shirts, elegant ties. With their pectorals swollen with pride and prejudice, their brains in their lunch box. Identity checks, sweeps. Orders ringing out on every side, all marching together in step, their movements like clockwork. Self-control, total composure. Theoretically, not one eyelash should flutter in fine weather or heavy storm. And yet . . .

Yacuba and his like can feel them through every pore even when they don't see them. If they're unlucky enough to bump into them on some out-of-the-way path, they make themselves scarce. These strange little games are incomprehensible to us. Like familiar but disturbing little fennecs, they roam around the outskirts of our cities in search of lord knows what, keeping their intentions to themselves, with their guns at their hips, their sunglasses firmly fixed on their nostrils. They concentrate on the right time to start tailing someone, arrest a crook, or smother the screams of the world. Most of the time they just watch them from a distance, deciphering the alphabet of their existence from afar. The waning light of the sun often makes them look sinister. And then all of a sudden some fellow in a worn-out cap comes into their line of vision singing the praises of Africola, the sparkling beverage known all over the world for its commercials and fierce competition with PopeSy. Sirens. Handcuffs. More sirens. The show's over already. A few steps away, the Abd el-Kader camp next to the Air Force wiretap center is swarming with people. A constant ballet of planes of all sizes and colors flying to or from the Persian Gulf, where military operations are taking place. Ah, Maya, where dromedaries used to snort and kids frolicked in the desert of monotheisms, today unbelievable storms are raging, and the local little tyrants have already left the ship to place themselves under our protection.

6 *Waiting for better days, a strange man in a dirty round cap hangs around town at the risk of his life.*

Now comes the rainy season, when leaves have little cracks around the edges, flowers wither, days grow somewhat shorter, and the air becomes mild and wet. People rub their hands and say "Good, it's getting cooler!" or "Let's take out the raincoats." In a few weeks, the rainy season will be here and the ground will congeal. And the trees will have drunk to their roots' content and the streets will look like dark chasms before the harmattan returns, before dew covers the leaves again and mimosas explode in flower beds and along pathways. People will rub their hands once again in the brightly shining sun, saying to themselves: "Nice weather, isn't it?"

The rain is here. The first mud. The Caucasians are turning over the soil of the yam fields in rhythm. All of them deep in mud. Same step, same sweat. The marsh birds in the Nile estuary count and recount themselves before migrating to the southern tip of the continent, much sunnier this time of year. A fog thick as the fog in Mombasa drops onto the flat country but spares the outskirts of Asmara for the moment. You gulp down your papaya juice. You hold out your coffee bowl to Doctor Papa as you watch the light gaining on the darkness through the picture window.

With his little round dirty cap on his head and a bag in his hand, he appeared, one humid afternoon, at the same time as big woolly storm clouds. He stationed himself there, diagonally opposite the house. Said nothing to anyone. Might not speak the language of the country. Doesn't want to, perhaps. They say he came out from behind the abandoned factory over there, near the railroad tracks that go off into the rapeseed fields and the blazing yellow of the alfalfa. They say he comes from very far away. He's the one who got off the bus. Who took the wrong line on a stormy evening. Who hasn't budged an inch since he's been here. Who's been hanging around here ever since. Who's surrounding himself with mystery. Who lives in silence, a silence from God knows where. He's the one who's trying to draw something in the dust with fingers long as eagle feathers. Who hiccups like someone who's had too much to drink. Who talks to no one, either because he doesn't speak the federal language properly or because the words that come out of his mouth remain inaudible.

We rub our eyes. We wonder, we're a bit worried. We know the people in this residential neighborhood, more or less. They have an address, a face and a name—unlike him. With his head buried in his shoulders, he looks at his feet. Then he readjusts his cap and gets up. Needs to stretch his legs? He pulls himself up, walks away proudly. With the confidence of someone wearing an embroidered silk fez. He won't get far. We'll find him in the same spot, or lying on the bench at the bus stop. Is this the end of the road for him? He's there, that's all. His silhouette has met the flame of our eyes, Maya.

When you speak to him, he doesn't really seem to be listening. You even wonder if he's heard anything. His dreamy, vacant, sullen ways make you fear for the worst. There! He's gone on a journey inside himself, you think. He no longer draws on the cigarette stuck between his lips like Joshua Ngouabi in *East of Bangui*. He's really gone. Where? He doesn't know, and doesn't know who's with him either. And then he starts mumbling something about the topic that came up a second earlier, and he really makes sense. He's back from his journey. He's here again, you know it instinctively. He'll be standing in front of the mosque on Ben Barka Street for the rest of the day. Silent as the grave, with his limp hand out. A long, bony hand.

Meanwhile, his silence tells you nothing. It's taking hold of his silhouette. It boxes him in, wraps itself around him. It's natural, it falls upon him at once, like the marks that will stay on the sidewalk for a few moments, like the fear of night that comes to us from way, way back, from the time of caves and the womb. The man in the cap is wordless, has no posterity. Sometimes a huge fire flares up in his eyes, his lips and his fists squeeze tight. He's afraid, it's coming back. If he died he would be buried the same day in accordance with the tradition in our lands. Borders are not for crossing, they're meant for very short stays. Fluid thread, human smears. The man in the dirty cap has bulging red eyes, skin rough as an elephant's. And when he tries to open his mouth, sadness drowns his eyes. Nothing in common with the junk sellers who send old, dilapidated Hippos and ancient second-hand Kudus to Europe. Nothing to do with the watchmen and apostles of the sects rapidly multiplying everywhere, playing on old fears, vying with each other in proclaiming the advent of a new era. The man without a shadow doesn't do that kind of thing, Maya. Not him. The mare of his desires has flown away without a whinny, sucked into other pastures. He whips the silence alone. It's a coat cut to measure for him. He recalls earlier times, times when there still was a time for him, over there. He's unshackled but lost in this urban dead end, once a mighty desert with its network of trails and its cohort of enchanting genies. He cracks his joints, feels the weight of his numb muscles, searches his surroundings in quest of a sign, vegetable or mineral—a gecko, a grain of millet, a roofing tile fallen with the last storm. He lives in this absence that is also his space, his identity card, his birth certificate. (The real one was purposely left in a slum in Yalta, or was it Königsberg?) His movements have neither beginning nor end. One of these days he'll go back inside himself, into the other side of his body. With no thirst and no appetite, he will stay there forever on a sleeping bag of ashes, with insomniac embers and chilling winds for companions. His eyes will become covered by an off-white veil reminiscent of the bloom on the purple grapes of Monastir. His skin will become extremely pale, his face crimson. Destiny will have played him like a violin.

The next day, the man in the cap is still rooted in the same spot. He's been looking at his feet for hours. He's alone with his talismans, amulets, and his bristling chin. Speaking to him would be like speaking to an unplugged computer, you probably tell yourself, and besides, it may be a good thing he's keeping his mouth shut. Nothing you can do will take him out of his bubble.

To the permanent dryness of their sky, people here have added miserly hearts and stingy speech. Stifling, strange, punctuated by tears, that's what home is like for them. So goes life, between their houses at the edge of the desert, wedged between the garbage dump and the soccer field where the roar of the crowd rises on Saturday afternoons. Here, what you don't say is more important than what you say. The clump of houses simmers in prudery, prejudice, and stuffy insularity. In living rooms, bedrooms, and above the beds, death invisibly expands and contracts its fleshless arms. Many are those who hole up inside for lack of faith in humanity. At least as many have bodies polluted by khat liquor, which dissolves the cells in a quicklime of ether and reduces them to deadly idleness. What will become of all that fresh energy, all those childhoods, all those sprouting lives, that young sap eager to rise? No animation or almost none in this pocket of green, except for the little electric car of the Federal Post Office coming and going, carrying the mail and African Express packages. More rarely gifts and flowers. The oasis dozes every single day, slowly sliding. Soon it will be overcome by the rigidity of death. We wish it a sound sleep.

7 *Legend has it that good Doctor Papa isn't fooled by the charms of the highway, rich in strange customs.*

Highway 99 leaves Djibouti to reach Dakar going east–west, crossing 122 at Niamey and connecting Tangiers to the Cape north–south; at twilight, it sinks into fog. Gradually, the headlights of the tank trucks and tractor-trailers, long as a subway train, make luminous blocks bright as comets that cut through this murk. The surprised drivers chant verses against fear and swerve over to the side to let the blacktop monsters go by. Identifiable by their olive skin, the Andalusian workers hide under the bridges, half to catch their breath, half to wolf down a goat sandwich. Glazed by the morning dew, wrung dry by the noonday sun, Highway 99 stretches out and expands under our eyes, reddened with wonder. With bamboos, banyans, eucalyptus, cannas, fig trees, rosebushes, and crape myrtles from the West Indies swelling up on either side, this road is a siren lying on a bed of greenery. A terrible enchantress full of grace and cunning. This beauty does not reveal herself to profane eyes, even though she arises from a pink mirage at dawn. All around her, the water takes on shimmering reflections, trails into the vanishing line. During the day, the sorceress embraces the mountains. At night she goes to sleep under the last shining of the moon, protected by the spirit of the place. From afar she attracts you like a magnet, Doctor Papa would note: he's a man who knows his highways and runaways. The enchantress has caressed the face of many a kid, swallowed up most of the Byelorussian road workers, who in fact hadn't been bold at all. Danger is on the prowl. All the time. They shoot first here; then the corpse is turned over and sometimes you hear "Aw, shucks! That was a friend!"

In which we can't resist the urge to borrow from the Chuvachian poet Guennedi Aïgui these strikingly true words: "When you come right down to it, what we call the people is nothing but the suffering of my mother." We also tell of the machine to produce dreams.

On the verge of dying, your mother has succeeded in passing the torch. She radiates the richness of those who know the violence of dying and the intensity of living. For you, she forms words as gentle as tenderness and dense as mourning. Her great camel eyes are almost lifeless. You say to yourself, in life you can gain everything and see it all disappear the next day. Life is a heavy spittoon hanging around our necks. And every day is "We'll see about that tomorrow." Your mother has the serene elegance of those for whom life is an intake of breath. She senses your alarm, the alarm of a child who no longer sees her parents in the same bed, who wonders in silence because she's afraid to raise questions: the answers would surely be too heavy for her shoulders. A child who knows for a fact that her Doctor Papa sleeps an uneasy sleep. Knows he wriggles about in the sheets of insomnia. Knows he must hear the faint hum of traffic on the highway more than two kilometers away and sense its little games, as it, too, pretends to fall asleep.

You are a child who knows that both her parents put on a show about everything. Accomplices in life as in death, with plenty of digs in the ribs and winks of the eye. Doctor Papa adjusts his breathing to the breathing of your ailing mother; he follows her deceptive respites, abrupt accelerations, sudden mood swings and calm spells. He lives with the terror that stirs the highway and the neighboring woods in the dead hours of dawn.

The neurologists in the Frantz Fanon Institute of Blida have come up with a dream-making machine that brings you whatever dreams you want while you sleep. Doctor Papa could treat himself to a dream of refreshing sleep, your mother the dream of a cure, you the dream of returning to your roots, and your neighbor the missionary dream of getting the pagans of California to return to the straight and narrow. Nobody has said yet when this machine will begin to function or how much it will cost to get one. The capacity to dream is not the sole privilege of painters, poets, and storytellers who make a profession out of it. It will be a good season for dreams of every size and color of the rainbow, you tell yourself, rubbing your hands. You're going to put on your fennec slippers and your gilded snake-charmer's cape, you are full of life and imagination, erasing the divide between brain and muscle, diving head first into the cavern of feelings and thoughts that is the birthplace of all the languages in the world.

Doctor Papa speaks a dead language, reduced to ashes, a language lighter than goose down. A language stuck in the past; its words and phrases have been fished from his own tank of memories. No present and no future. No regrets, no malice. As the days passed, his memories have taken on the shape of time itself. Doctor Papa has aged just as much. His beard has grown all by itself, long and thick. Longer than the beard of the prophet Enoch, who's supposed to have lived more than 365 years, according to Genesis. Remember, Malaïka, Enoch is, like Elijah, one of those extremely rare prophets never to have known death. After years of research by all the scholars, all the theologians and their faithful followers, Enoch was thought to have completely vanished. And then they actually found him, do you know where? In Ethiopia, of course! Centuries later, it was also Ethiopia that welcomed the exiled young prophet Muhammad (may his name be praised!) with all the honors due him. Now there's something to fan the fires of the imagination for centuries to come in the Vatican or Medina and create an influx of immigrants, don't you think, Maya?

Under your very eyes, Doctor Papa has withdrawn into an endless, bottomless silence. He sits in his rocking chair with his eyes on the sky, his beard thicker than usual. He remains deaf to your questions. You would like to remind him that absorbing someone else's words, gestures, and body is the only way to be fully oneself. But you will do nothing of the kind. All you'll do is listen to his muttering. See how this house hasn't changed since the time when you took your first steps while he was dozing off on the velvet couch, rocked to sleep by the music of Abdullah Ibrahim (the super-talented child of the Cape), Oum Kalsoum, and Franklin Boukaka. In that sugary carefree state, the world fluctuated between waking and sleep. Thoughts, feelings, and visions fused together. You would imagine yourself as an angel: soft, silken wings sprouted from your armpits. You were an angel, Maya, both light and vigorous. You were as fresh as a newborn butterfly in the pure air. All softness the moment before, you would change on the spot: a firm fruit sporting all the colors of existence. In your family perhaps more than in others, everything was an excuse for passion and excess. Everything rose high, words and sounds and even the larva wrenched from its dull sluglike existence, from the dead water of frogs and toads. Then peace would return, silence would take over once again. Music reconciled you, always.

You watch Doctor Papa doze. You put down your brushes, you take a rest in the armchair under the glass roof after your work. You hesitate between a bowl of hot *kinkeliba* and a glass of iced *bissap*. It is already black as pitch outside, for you didn't see time zipping by. With a swish of your wings, you go through the other side of the looking glass in order to go out there, where it's still broad daylight. Where the whole world is quiet, hanging on your every word, just waiting for you to come. Gradually, the murmur of a crystal fountain from which the purest water gushes forth. You came into this world at a moment just like this one. You have been gliding serenely, swimming in the starry world of dreams ever since.

Childhood is a time of wonder, the season when the soul expands. You have to turn yourself into words, words from the mouth of that very same childhood, to resist the grim reaper with his bony hips who drags his scepter around the house, counts the days that remain to your mother, threatens Doctor Papa; every morning, after his bowl of coffee, he goes up to the room where your mother has lived as a recluse these past years. A corridor, white as death, separates their two bedrooms upstairs. At the end of the hall is the small bathroom with a wallpaper pattern of magnified butterfly wings. Every time the conversation returns to your mother's shaky health (and how to avoid the topic, for that is practically your main subject of conversation) Doctor Papa remains on safe ground and his words lose their effect. The grim reaper watches over your exchanges, keeping them in his nets, bogged down in the swamp of endless reiterations and repeats.

Every passing day brings its share of dead leaves granted by the wind to hardened city people like you: leaves heavy with dust, trampled on by people more cheerful than your distressed dad. He is the only one who wants to hold on to the memory of former days, to keep the key to the past, to navigate between "yesteryear" and "days of yore." Everyone else submits to the tick-tock of daily life, the order of life that pulses with each passing second: cry, all right; then forget and live. But he does only what suits him, wandering off gladly into the strands of yesterday. And after all, your mother isn't dead yet, Maya! The thought of seeing her go enrages him, turns him into a mad dog without master or bone. Irascible. Exhausted. He is already dozing; sliding along, dead wood. Drowning in melancholy. Only your stories, your words, your letters can keep something like a flame alive in him. You learned that he spent a lot of time reading your letters when you went off to study art in the university: with the lights burning in his room all night long, he pored over each one of your letters, keeping away the grim reaper with his fresh-shaved eyebrows and his ankles rattling against each other in the rhythm of his steps; Doctor Papa bristled in front of him like a big cat defending her cub.

Now he has fallen asleep. You go down to the living room. "Get out right away. Go. Go to your studio," he had whispered before taking his pills. A few moments went by. Did you really hear that howl or was it the sound of broken glass? You look out the window. Nothing is moving outside. It can only be coming from upstairs. From the depths of his chest, in a place where feelings and self-control mix, came an irrepressible sound, a moan, the cry of an animal wounded for the rest of its life. You charge up the stairs. He has collapsed, he's sleeping like an angel. Where did that howling come from? Was it a cry of deliverance? You go back to your brushes and your reed quills. Overwhelmed by grief, tears lining his face, Doctor Papa seems to have found new provisions of serenity for the night.

Outside, this small corner of urban jungle is curling up in the arms of the rising dawn. It is already time for you to go up to bed.

9 *The tales of our travelers back from terrae incognitae are enough to keep you from sleeping. But Gondwana welcomes you with open arms.*

Twenty-three. That is the number of slave ports in Eritrea, Nubia, Somalia, and all of blessed northeast Africa. Ports where Yacuba and his like are breaking their backs today. Ports once watered with the sweat and blood of bold workers from the West, following the example of Batavian produce vendors, Icelandic fishermen, Basque fish dryers, Sardinian stonecutters, Moldavian ironworkers, hired gunsmiths and horsemen, Romanian tanners, Calabrian dyers, Slovenian bear trainers, Uzbek gravediggers, Maltese falcons, Texan pawnbrokers, Serbian eunuchs, Mongol shamans, masons from the distant Baltic, ash-blond slaughterers from the Rhineland, and Provençal trouvères, some of whom have walked dry-shod across the Red Sea. And then ports living for centuries off ivory from all over Europe, especially the Slavic countries, carried to the bottom of Africa by way of Asia Minor, Palestine, and happy Arabia.

And so, from this centuries-old trade, from these trading posts and grain and sugar cane plantations, memory has retained nothing. Few traces in stone in Asmara, Massawa, Obock, Port Said, or Bengazi—the oldest cities in the region, from which African civilization sent its missionaries, scholars, and geographers. Following Nzila Kongolo Wa Th'iongo (1786–1852), once so popular in the court of the unpredictable monarch Kodjo Alemjoro, author of the classic *An Evening on the Danube*, travel writers back from terrae incognitae have darkened page after page with "exotic screwing," the urge to "wash away the equatorial fogs," to "plunge their weapon into the mouth of alabaster-skinned houris" and to swing their navels to the rhythm of "bronze-belled mules." I still get hard thinking about it, but let us move on.

African man felt sure of himself very early on. He saw himself as a superior being on this earth, without equal, since he was separated from other peoples and races by an infinitely vast space. He elaborated a system of values in which his throne is at the top. The others—natives, barbarians, primitives, pagans (almost always white)—are reduced to the rank of pariahs. The universe seems to have been created only to raise him up, to celebrate him.

Did you know, Maya, that at the beginning there was only one continent surrounded by seas, Pangaea, that would split into fragments at the end of the Jurassic era? Africa was located at the south of a single block called Gondwana. Later on, Gondwana would break up into many drifting continents, but only Africa would remain stable, at the center of the world. Remember the main point: Africa was already at the center, and still is. Nothing has changed since then, or very little. Under the visible crust of the Earth, there is still an underground world, swarming with life. What is life, if not organisms appearing and taking their energy from the food chain—or if you will, Maya, all-out predation? Nothing has changed; geology proves this. Just think a moment, Maya, of the artificial lakes we have made, their waters still flowing with atavistic regularity over Quaternary wadis. Think of the countless fossils periodically uncovered by sandstorms. Finally, think of those millions of grass, cactus, or orchid seeds waiting peacefully for the drop of water that will transform them from an inert chrysalis to the vegetable and floral state. Between two rocks standing like the forefingers of the law, hundreds, thousands, of insects, small rodents, and tiny reptiles slither around, hanging on to puny stalks—stalks of thirst-quenching green.

10 *On the author's latest inspired invention for entertaining the reader.*

Armstrong, I am not black
My skin is white
It's a real lack
For singing hope
No use seeing birds and sky
Nothing, nothing there is bright
Angels? Nope
My skin is white

That's a song of Claude Nougaro's, right? Are you still listening to it inside your studio, Maya dear? Nougaro, the notes on the record jacket clearly say, is a Caucasian songwriter of the Provençal race who celebrated our greatest musicians, as this complaint clearly shows; it was found in a shack in Toulouse, ravaged since then by the ethnic warfare opposing the Patriotic Movement for the Liberation of Occitania (PMLO) and the Republican troops from Paris. Troops who had lost Alsace, Lorraine, the Vendée, Brittany, Savoy, and Provence. Ah, all those mouths we have to feed in fair weather or khamsin! The schoolchildren will launch another "Operation Bowl of Millet-Okra Sauce" this year, your mother would sigh from her sickbed.

11 *On a few tricks and traps of History.*

The great names of Federal history have abandoned their majestic postures as statues, caryatids, obelisks, and bronzes erected at the four corners of our cities to end up as little Jesuses in bell jars selling at five guineas a piece. These trinkets are all the rage with foreign tourists, especially with Brazilians, Haitians, Jamaicans, Cubans, Caribbeans, and Indians.

It is painful for all of us to see Nelson Mandela, Haile Selassie, Zumbi, Julius Nyerere, Sarraouina, Ousmane dan Fodio, or the giant Muhammad Ali as captives in these little plastic boxes, standing on a tiny little mound of sand, without an ounce of the cosmetic canonization usually bestowed on the illustrious dead. How can you explain this lack of interest for our historic heritage, Maya? It leaves me dumbfounded, confounded and aghast. The Axum obelisk, over seventeen hundred years old, needs immediate restoration—you know that. This twenty-five-yard high giant bore witness to the time when Axum was the capital of an empire that reigned over the Horn of Africa, from Sudan to Yemen on the other bank of the Red Sea. Why, then, is it left coated with soot like that? Why do pigeons and pollution take all the blame? Meanwhile our historians, lavish with their smiles, never tire of crowing over its symbolism. Of describing that period as the apogee of a country overflowing with ivory, gold dust, slaves, aromatic herbs, and emeralds for trade with the other powers of the era. Of reminding us that the monument was built in the fourth century, under the reign of King Ezana—called the Divine Lord of Ethiopia—to serve as his tombstone. Or pointing out the delicacy of its body—you won't disagree about that, will you?—wrenched out of a block of basalt by artistic hands. Or emphasizing its exact location in what was then the sacred wood of the city. Or swooning over the Ethiopians' love for "God's Flute" (the expression comes from a local poet). And finally, acknowledging its popularity across the ages and its status as a national icon.

Before touching the base of the obelisk, feeling and caressing it all over, you had admired its shapes and proportions on banknotes, stamps, clothing, and official documents. If anyone asked for your opinion, Malaïka, you would have made a real clay coat for it in the Federal colors (green, yellow, and red), the finest and worthiest possible, for the monuments one has loved should last, should live as they have lived. "But what can you do? Everything's going to the dogs," Mama would sigh before slipping into a coma. She is never to recover from her sorrow, for she will trade what is transitory for eternity. Any day is a good day to be born. Any day is a good day for dying.

12 *In which we also tell of a gazelle-skin jacket and ebony jeans.*

Mother, I'm running after the smell of your breast, this is what you tell yourself. I run after your face, your touch, the caress of your eyes. One day I will be yours once again, like the veil of your eyelids, this is what you keep repeating to yourself. I will cross the seas, the oceans, and deserts if necessary. I will be your shadow, your sweat, your fragrance. I will cover your bones with a clod of earth, earth blessed by my steps from the time I came and went in our garden, where I would lose myself in play. I would run and nestle into your breast as soon as you came home from work. My heart would be beating against your fingers. I would drink down your smile, intoxicated by the shining of your lily-white teeth. Your first words were always for me. Yes, for me alone.

The house you grew up in has remained discreet, no display worthy of the luxurious Moroccan *ryads* with wrought-iron balconies hidden behind thick leaves that are found in some suburbs. No opulent mosaics or rococo chandeliers. No gate opened by remote control as in the home of people who weave the threads of their lives on a web of boredom and fear. Still less of showy or cumbersome things, except for the huge painting that takes up the whole main wall of the living room: a reproduction of Mansour Fall's *Turkish Bath*. The furniture, the engravings and the invitation cards displayed over the fireplace, the photographs stowed pell-mell in shoeboxes, nothing in all this shows any character or sets it apart from the tapir tusks and warthog heads hanging in the living rooms of nearby houses. The heart of your childhood mythology is really only a little middle-class house with a big garden, the kind found in any corner of our urban jungle, in any megalopolis of our standardized world, in which reality is a scene in a film where anything can happen at any time.

As an only child, you spent your childhood inventing brothers and sisters, do you remember now, Malaïka? What concerns you is not the faraway world with its strange people and unpredictable catastrophes, but the ordinary course of the human condition. What concerns you is the next five minutes, the fate of the man in the dirty cap, whom you haven't seen for the past few days. The threat is in the present. Nobody can feel safe, not outside in the underbrush or inside the enclosure of our homes. Something can cut through the scene, or life, like a stray bullet. That thing can occur at any moment, shake the foundations of the world. That's what we call life. It includes shouts, faces, and sorrows, too. What you see depicted in your paintings takes a bit of this existential weight off you. You are facing the essence of suffering studded with tiny instants of happiness.

Maya, do you sometimes ask yourself "Who am I?" And is the person you see every morning in the mirror—that double, that twin—so familiar? Or is she already taking up too much space? What is she plotting behind your back? What is she saying about you? Do you think she's going to stay put, tired and full like lion cubs after their feast? She is waiting only for you, waiting so ardently it has become an obsession, her reason for living, her destiny. She watches your every move. She sees you as a rival, a competitor, or worse, a mortal enemy. She will jump at your throat at the first occasion. You seriously think she'll give you presents, that she'd give her life for yours, just like that? You're really naïve. If a photographer were there, he would reveal the schemes of the double crouched behind the mirror. He would capture every move she made and bring you the evidence in his negatives. For once, you'd stand there speechless before the mass of evidence, dumfounded by the deceitful, underhand nature of your alter ego. "Who can you trust, I wonder," you would have sighed, as you faced the facts. You would stop believing in chance. You would feel more Lilliputian than Miriam Makeba in the hand of King Kong. (Now that was a hell of a great film! I forgot its name, but never mind.) You'd tell yourself I'm humble, I can't possibly provoke so much violence. No point dirtying your ax with my blood, no need to waste a bullet on me. The game isn't worth the candle.

You would also tell yourself that living is a hard job, but a wonderful one. Relieved, you would get dressed in a gazelle-skin jacket, ebony jeans, and a mauve tie. And you would go out to face the day, with all the challenges it brings. You'd go see if that other guy, the one in the filthy cap, the man who has lost his shadow, is still wandering around out there. That's the way things always end up with you.

13 *Because it never rains but it pours.*

On your way to the Maryse Condé Bookstore on the corner of Fifth Avenue and Samory-Touré Street, you pass more and more desirable coconut-skinned girls, dragging their high heels in front of the Hérémakhonon Metro Station. They are young women your age—as you've reflected many times. The ones who're given away to be married at twelve or thirteen in the slums of old Europe and the whole Northern hemisphere, from Vladivostok to San Francisco, Doctor Papa would have mumbled before sinking back into his silence, right, Maya? Held against their will in the discreet alcoves of our cities and ranches by an invisible tarantula.

Their frightened fawn eyes break your heart. They make men happy—the ones who confuse pleasure with spreading their cum. The ones who think their prick is a stem, an axis, an axle. And that stirs your heart. For a few guineas, respectable grandfathers—august worthies—come to die and be reborn inside them. They know everything about the charms and folds of these women brought from the banks of the Volga on muleback or towed from the thick forests of Thracia or Saxony. Their electric blue eyes, their long blonde locks, their discreet chests and flat buttocks delight everyone, from CEOs to the unemployed, from princes of oil to kings of electronics, ulemas or lay people. With goose steps and bustard feathers, they slip into Bedouin tents. Human landscapes right there where you can touch them. The fogs and mists wrapped around the Alps and Transylvania suddenly drop onto our solar streets, while snow trots along with muffled steps. Pleasure, babbling, rapture and screams. Our Bedouins in their birthday suits prance on their Crimean camels, their nostrils in the wind. Our Bedouins sprawling on rugs of flesh and mingled secretions like those distant Carthaginians, or splashing in jacuzzis with their dicks in their hands. "Your ass is my road to Damascus," concedes a trembling old man. And what about the men who sell them, give them away, subcontract them? Circus performers looking for an audience, revolutionaries with multiple allegiances to various acronyms, grumpy braggarts boasting in oppressed idioms, wandering monks traveling with their nuns in worn-out boots, counterfeiters with Stalin mustaches, nameless pimp-lords, and so on.

In which, having left the Chari and Zambesi of her childhood, our heroine finds herself a prisoner in an extraordinary palace.

You've just had this dream: you're a prisoner. And not just any prisoner. You are held by an Ashanti prince straight from a marvelous fairy tale. Sequestered in a palace so beautiful you'd risk damnation for it. You walk around under its green dome capped by a silver horseman defying lightning. A captive in this labyrinth of ninety passages, imagined by the mathematical genius Adel Aïtchine (1879–1955), a native of Upper Egypt. And it so happens that Ayissi, a princess coiffed with a brilliant tiara, is in the same situation. In the span of one night, she tells you the story of her long, dangerous, tortuous life.

She was truly pampered. She had asked her suitor for the most sumptuous gifts and received them. Jewels, precious stones, perfumes, flowers and fruits from all over, great vintages, rare fabrics, essential oils. And the lightest taffetas, and the most shimmering kente dresses. She possessed all that the Creator—glory be to Him alone!—can grant us in this world. But with no inner flame and an empty heart, she languished. She thought and thought, for days and nights. There was one solution, if only to patch her life together—for it was on the brink of fraying apart. She consulted the greatest divines in Farafina. All of them pointed her to the same path of blood and sex. She finally set out to entrust her body to a young Adonis, handsome as an Abyssinian negus and calm as a Chokwe mask. One of the co-wives, perhaps the oldest, with her jealousy slung across her shoulder, gave away the game. Ayissi was immediately punished by Sankofa, her princely spouse. From that moment on, she would wander in this labyrinth where the bloodiest plots are hatched.

Your dream stops short. You wake up covered with sweat, Maya. You are hot, you are afraid. You're breathing hard. Very quickly, you come to, and something reassuring is born inside you. Memories flow in, soon to be followed by other reminiscences. A little smile appears on your face and soon grows broader and broader. You are soothed, like the sparrow plunging its head into the mist of a stream without caring about the eagle that could swoop down on it like night on day. You get up.

It is still night. Fireflies and beetles rub their wings and hum. The stars are on sentry duty till dawn, until the night birds cease to disturb the ordinary existence of hominids. Their peace is troubled by that old fear from the distant past. From the time they lived on gathering and fishing in a world rustling with big cats. On the way back from gathering honey, the last one in the single file was devoured by leopards and man-eating lycaons. Ever since, the imminent danger of sudden, violent death has permeated our minds. Worse still: men remain prey to their desires; the inner storm in their entrails imposes its rules, its burning dreams and the urgent ticking of its clock. They are strangers and strange ever since they left their mother's womb and its amniotic bath. They still have nostalgia for that oasis. Once they have left the Zambezi and the Chari of childhood, they become inconsolable, like cherubs whose toys have been trampled on. They flare up cyclically like ships in the paintings of Tahir Ibn Bakri. If yesterday's paradise smelled of Zanzibar roses and Meroe myrrh, they survive here below shut in their foul-smelling burrow, wanting nothing, saying nothing, anxious to merge back into the primal silence. Constantly fearful, their hearts more sensitive than African radar. Their existence, or more precisely their hegira, is always knocked about, bumped around and pushed off its path by faithless, pitiless Barbary tanks.

Your mother is dying, her name soon to be engraved on the tombstone. Now you endow her with an abundance of virtues, and above all with tenderness. From now on, you'll have to stop talking of her in the past tense. You will only evoke her in the present, as firm as the earth beneath our feet. Kaddish for the adored mother now lighter than a soap bubble; soon she will have joined the recumbent statues that populate the cemeteries and watch us from afar. She will have done well to leave this world and its morgue, right, Maya? Lying in her bed for long, pitiful years, she suffered martyrdom in secret. She stopped talking a few weeks ago. She flaps her lips like a dying fish when the pain becomes unbearable. She expects nothing anymore, no remedy, no miracle. She knows all there is to know about hospitals: the IVs, the boiled meat, white walls, medicinal smells, squealing of carts in the halls, the phony pleasant faces of the nurses, the mad doctors who insist on examining her insides. Enough already!

Once she's gone, she'll go plant her tent in the stillness of the tomb. No need to age on the stalk, to stir up fear inside those around you, maintain at all costs a body weakly surviving inside a failing spirit. The organs can still function for a few weeks on the crutches of modern medicine, but they'll lack lubrication, alchemy, invigorating breath. And that's something you can't buy, my dear Maya! Medicine can't eclipse death by giving it a coat of bright paint. It is incapable of fanning the embers of the desire to live, the projections of self, the arrows of the imagination at work. The thousand ways of being a human among your loved ones.

15 *Without making a song and dance about it, the author informs the reader about the latest fashion in our excellent federation.*

An exotic new trend, peddled by fashion designers like Léon Lafricain, Chris Seydou, and Zachary Onana, DJs like Afrika Bambaata, Mwalimu Haruna, Skip Gates, or Irele Abiola, has descended upon our lands. Some rebel, talking of poisonous illnesses, foreign and infectious bodies, unheard-of punishments. The problem lies elsewhere. The worm is in the fruit. The canons of beauty will be shaken for a long, long time. Our ebony, mahogany, almond, chocolate, henna, sienna-skinned women—are they all forgotten? Rolling hips, generous bosoms, fleshy thighs, exciting curves, full mauve lips—all rejected? Callypigian muses, scornfully dismissed? Kaolin smiles—completely erased? Our creators have eyes only for stems of alabaster with lingerie-pink cheekbones and flat butts. You can just picture it, Maya! Pleated bubus, draped djellabas, wraparound haiks, majestic *gandouras*, raffia and straw, ivory and amber, muslin and cotton, cowries and tortoise shells—vanished, all gone! Now is the time of jacket and pants, gray suits, ties, long skirts, sheath dresses, and tuxedos.

No wonder our sisters get depressed by this craze, by the invasion of cute little things picked up in the underbrush of Rome, Paris, Moscow, or New York. Hard to avoid those painted creatures striking the poses of a Turkish harem, those eyes burning or running with mascara, those echoing hard high heels clacking on our pavements all night long. Crippled with tranquilizers, they nod off, force a grin and simper. G-strings and pig-white velvet bikinis show off on our beaches, from Alexandria to Conakry, from Luanda to Essaouira. One step forward, three steps back. Swaying hips. Rubbing and snuggling.

Cum spreading and ass plowing right there on the sand. Farts smelling of boiled cabbage and marijuana. Bloody pus in the stools.

And thus, these *African Queens* in impala-skin dresses encrusted with studs and pieces of mother-of-pearl or ivory, part high-class hookers, part frivolous scum, vow to take the Devil by the horns. To behave as worthy descendents of the famous Amazons who strutted around in the court of King Behanzin. To reverse the trend, or at least contain it for now. Before the neguses, ulemas, various clergies and *ngandas*, zealots of redemption, religious reform and patriotism, descend from Mount Nouba for the occasion and make it their business. As usual, they'll start whining that a thousand hydras are strangling our civilization and recommend that these immaculately white nymphets striped with vice be deported immediately. They will gain wide approval in this country, so insular and so intoxicated with itself, where hardly 14 percent of its citizens have a passport to travel abroad.

The *African Queens* know that their mission is certainly difficult, but it is really an act of the greatest patriotism. Time is short, Maya. They begin by setting up security perimeters in big cities, investigate at length before tackling lawless zones, shady hotels, guerilla camps, bordellos, and shebeens for illegal immigrants. They make a list of suspects, uncover underground networks. They're scary, too. And all the ill-dressed, ill-born, ill-fed people, the alienated and the maniacs of the vulva, go to ground once again.

And now they're extending their investigations to the sweet citadel of Tadjoura, the Mecca of the film industry and leisure on Haile Wade hill. Ah, Tadjoura! Tadjoura, its bay, its wide avenues lined with royal palm trees, its exquisite movie stars, its dream location. Tadjoura, the bluest bay in the country, shaded by huge rows of carob trees, bougainvilleas, tamarinds, jacarandas, pepper trees, mango trees, and a multitude of trees brought back from the four corners of the globe and acclimated effortlessly: a small paradise for the superrich, pallid stars. It would make Sun City jealous. Tadjoura lives out its quiet days, except for the usual frenzied onlookers in the marina reserved for the film industry, the reassuring potpourri of canned music and the sirens of ambulances. Fervent fans gather there every day of the year, lit up at the view of an anorexic star, an alcoholic screenwriter fond of aloe liqueur, or an erotomaniac videomaker with jumbled speech.

At nightfall Tadjoura becomes Tadjoura once again and regains its legendary calm. No more flashily dressed pimps, just the occasional roar of a powerful car and a supersonic Malcolm X. The city is cradled by the narrow artificial river that squeals with pleasure, winding along the left bank right near the heart of the old town and rolling its eyes of illusion. This fortress of felicity, this Salem on the Red Sea, falls asleep, sated and serene, as soon as the last day-visitor has left. And yet.

The city cleanup machine is on the move. Get rid of the undeveloped, the destitute, the beggars, the refugees and prostitutes with bruised and swollen flesh—this is the new political deal spread about by great minds of the caliber of Professor Emeritus Garba Huntingabwe, that unforgettable voice of a talk show host, of a cigarette roller turned mandarin. The *African Queens* also have the ear of Dr. Edmond Abu Chanab, of the Brazzaville Academy of Theology, who siphons up Finnish and Lithuanian women with fjord-colored eyes the way one tamps down a pipe. Who's mad about milky palpitating flesh, bulbous and overflowing with corruption, fountains of youth offered up not just for our eyes to see.

Everyone has his little weakness, right, Maya? It would be foolish not to touch it, squeeze it, knead it. No big deal. Besides, it's cheap. Prowling around, initiating an enigmatic, totemic dance, eyes riveted on the fleshy, veiny envelope soaked with water and blood. One's eyes become a second pair of hands. Desire to the wind, you rush forward, you let yourself be overwhelmed by the tick-tock of blood beating from the underground springs of the body. The ultimate call, the horse-back ride, the fireworks. The full stomach rumbling in concupiscent pleasure. The frenzy of the unbridled flesh, the wild thermal party that unites and separates bodies. The heart hammering, hiccupping, beating out the rhythm and roll of the hips. Transports of the humors. The Big Bang localized in the genitals. The soufflé collapses. Calm returns, padded in cotton wool. A little breeze, as invigorating as the first cigarette of the day. And you can bet your bottom dollar that the carousel, the heart-rending airs of the balalaika, the sound of suction and skins rubbing against each other, will start up again soon.

But how can you take a thorn from your side without spilling blood and tears? Should one hide, act openly? The sadistic methods of Messrs. Huntingabwe and Abu Chanab know no bounds: rinsing your face with an icy sponge for the time it takes to recover between two blows to the solar plexus. Now you've collapsed into a couch designed by Nka. That's the whole trick of those experts who change their views like chameleons according to the power they have at the moment while turning their back on the sufferings of Christians tormented by poverty and shame, placed in the psychologically untenable position of illegal immigrants, phony refugees or phony converts.

But hey, time is short. I must go on with my story.

In which we also tell of the hummingbird's song and the crash of earthquakes.

You've had another strange dream that left you in a cold sweat. You were alone without Doctor Papa; you have to watch over him constantly, ever since your poor mother fell into a coma. You were alone, and what's worse, without a single story in your head and without an audience. A Scheherazade in tears. So you were alone in the midst of a world finally straightened out by a right-handed God thanks to a planetwide tectonic drift, since the present world, ruled over by our left-handed God, doesn't satisfy anyone any more—as each of us feels every day in the depths of his soul. Even the tree-dwelling apes of Mongolia no longer get anything out of it. A thoroughly revised world, one of those magic tricks that our artistic God (or Devil) can play so masterfully. Hummingbird's song and the crash of earthquakes. The South becoming the North, or vice-versa; rivers, highways, gas pipelines, and forests following the same mad flight, or vice-versa. The fevers of damp Asia end up in the northern plains of Canada. The Cormoros Archipelago grazing on the Siberian tundra. Deserts, famines, wars, miseries, and viruses all making the same migration under the eyes of the stars, which, defying the constraints of the laws of gravitation, have no need to descend into the terrestrial arena.

Whew, you've awakened, covered with sweat. You have caught your breath, looked at the alarm clock. You have recovered your spirits, and naturally, you're relieved. You'll have a cup of Neguscafé before facing the difficult task of living.

And you remembered what you were told when you were a child. Once you're lying in your grave, an angel comes down as soon as the last shovelful of earth has been thrown on your body wrapped inside an opaline winding sheet. An endless interrogation begins with the arrival of Izrael, the second angel, who always places himself at your left in a position diametrically opposite the first, who places himself at your right side. Questions will cascade from both sides; they'll put your whole life through the mill. You will suffocate in your grave, but in the dark your senses will get sharper with time. You will be constantly tormented. You will hear squeaks, far off at first, then nearer and nearer. No, you're not dreaming; you will no longer have the leisure or the capacity to dream. What you hear, what you see and what you are now feeling in your own flesh really are rats, snakes, and bats. Swarming worms are attacking you. You are racked by tetanic convulsions. You are pure pain. You have no room to curl up your legs or stretch out your arms. You're done for. Nobody will come to help you.

Every paradise has its serpent, says a Lesotho proverb. Yet all human beings dream of silken beds, of rivers of milk and honey. All of them see themselves covered in gold and swathed in incense. Welcomed by houris with swaying hips and big black eyes, like the ones found in icons of the Abyssinian church. The first feeling of the holy goes far, far back, well before their own birth, well before their ancestors were born. Thunderstruck, they ceaselessly repeat the ninety-nine divine names, kneel on prie-dieus, shed hot tears for the Virgin, turn prayer mills, or melt into the silence to join the cosmic flux. Between the womb and the coffin we see the same passion, the same questioning, the same rites. Yes, every paradise has its serpent, but which one is at the controls? The distant paradise with its promises, its fine-horned cows, its perfumed gardens full of cool flowing springs, its thorough-breds, its banquets and submissive servants? Or the serpent of reality, here and now with each and every one of us? All united in the same dance, one identical step, one sweat. All talking and making others talk, all living and making others live. All clerks of the court of time, which goes inexorably by.

17 *You can bet that Helvetian's going to die.*

They found Yacuba this morning, or was it last evening? The police found only a few scarce clues: his dirty cap and a letter to his Zurich family that was never sent. Peanuts, in short. The investigation was wrapped up in a hurry by a pimply intern from Arusha.

An individual by the name of Maximilien Geoffroy de Saint-Hilaire, born in the canton of Zurich, date unknown, a carpenter working in Asmara, Eritrea, United States of Africa, was found deceased in a dead end adjoining Toussaint-Louverture Street.

A quiet dead end, far from the night streets that breathe, vibrate, and chant with feverish vitality. It appears that he died late last night. Left there with the nape of his neck flat on the ground. Died of neglect, emptied of his blood. Wallet in place, pockets untouched. No obvious motive. No witness, no fuss. No police record. The intern closed the case, concluding that the origin of death was probably a fight that ended badly.

But you have a flair for these things, Maya. You and I both noticed that the crime weapon bears the stamp of the criminal, or criminals. How could the Arusha clue-hunter pay no attention to such a signature? Was it lack of experience? Laziness? Or both? The rest is hardly negligible either. The position of the wax-colored corpse. The puddle of blood and its layout. The high-heeled shoe. The large hole in the right temple. It took an awful lot of work to finish him off like that. Kaddish for good old Maximilien Geoffroy de Saint-Hilaire.

Admit it: you were shaken by this crime and the dead-end investigation. As usual, you've retreated inside yourself. You resolutely repressed the motives for your dull anger, Maya. Sickened by the squalid, over-crowded conditions of the illegal immigrants, be they Caucasians or Martians, their hobo's life made of stops and starts, whether they come from Boston, Besançon, or Bucharest. Shaken, in fact enraged, you will keep silent for a long time before emerging again. Once again, you will take advantage of the emulative virtues of art. You'll lower your head and throw yourself into your work the way others lose themselves in the whites of their beloved's eyes.

As an only child, so different from your loving and aging parents, your main playground was school up to that unfortunate afternoon. Yet you've put school aside for a while to follow the paths of the Internet, you stay away from the ever-numerous family festivities, including Kwanzaa, so sacred in our households. Including Chanukah. You're getting an education all by yourself, you think, no doubt minimizing the support you get from your parents, as all children do who catch the images chance blows their way. Remember, it was in the company of your father the pediatrician that you noticed for the first time how a leaf comes off its branch. And it certainly was your mother who made you aware of the moment an ovary produces an egg. Do you really think you learned everything all by yourself, Maya? Ah, how ungrateful children are! Nothing new about that.

You're not so different from the birdbrained kids who demonstrate in front of McDiops and Sarr Mbock coffeehouses or rip out genetically modified rice plants in Libyan and Namibian rice paddies under the pretext that these products of high added value are harmful to health, attack the ozone layer, and pollute the planet. Resigned to their posi-tion as flunkeys and beasts of burden, the rag pickers of Vancouver and the convicts of Melbourne are delighted to gulp down Kalahari rice and Sahel beef sandwiches under the McDiop logo. Some of these young people with long dirty hair and hideous piglike snouts even take the joke so far as to shout "End African domination!" and others, "Another world is possible!"

You were burning to join them, Maya, and you did! But did you understand a single solitary word of their intergalactic speeches, their desire to conjugate the near and the far, their hazy alchemy between the universal and the local? Think globally, act locally—now there's an immensely stupid idea! Didn't Ibn Battuta do exactly the same thing in his time? And did Wole Soyinka wait for the ukases of this gang of hotheads and small-time gladiators to accomplish what he had to do? You can't hide the fact that your little pals co-opt any solidarity or individual action so they can reduce their subversive character by making them part of their great flow of chatter. Don't they know they owe their health and prosperity to the gray shadows dressed in rags who cross the Mediterranean to sell themselves to Transvaal manufacturers or the Nouakchott merchant marine? Charity begins at home. Open your eyes wide, Maya. Look around!

18 *In which it turns out that one is often
disappointed by one's neighbors, even
though they're people just like you and me.*

Awakened by a sense of foreboding heavier than mercury, he remains immobile for a long time, in a state of stupor, struck by aphasia. Before he opened his eyes he had the distinct feeling that familiar hands, gentle, firm hands, were pulling his blanket down. Hands that were taking him somewhere and were no longer there when he opened his eyes. He starts breathing again, lies down and stretches out down to the tips of his toes.

Outside, the urban jungle is no more than a backdrop covered by the white fur of routine. He'll have to try hard to get out of bed, find his slippers, take a few steps into the kitchen. The rest will demand still more willpower: to pour half a liter of mineral water into the plastic cylinder of the coffee pot, take out a bowl, dump in a spoonful of Neguscafé, sit down and open the newspaper immediately: the AAP (All African Publications) guarantees delivery before 6:00 a.m. to fifty-six million subscribers on the East Coast alone. The beeping of the coffeepot will pull him out of his drowsiness. He'll get up, push the chair aside, bring the boiling water back to the table, help himself while glancing out the window for the first time. He'll bring this bitter drink to his lips, his eyes will slide over the first page and stop for a handful of seconds on Abel Mvondo's editorial, always so fair and balanced.

This is when you'll make your appearance. You'll plant a big noisy kiss on his bald forehead. He'll sigh with pleasure, but complain a bit, too.

"What is your mother suffering from, exactly?" begs your neighbor, a psychoanalyst with mother envy, an inveterate gossip with a mania for weather reports. All the misery in the world that lands on her couch isn't enough to quench the unhealthy curiosity of this woman. A woman whose ideals have been amputated, who spends her time examining the wrinkles on her face in all kinds of mirrors: the swing-mirror in her bedroom, the pointed mirror in her bathroom, the picture window on her porch, the shiny enamel of the kitchen sink, the 27 × 27 screen of her Atlas TV, the rear-view mirror of her little five-HP Hippo, the chrome of her desk on the thirty-fourth floor of the Steve Biko Centro, the reflectors of the Matuba nightclub, the zinc bar of the Tropicana tea house, the muddy waters of the Blue Nile, in the lobby of the Pushkin Galeries and the mouths of people conversing with her. Mirrors, all of them.

Your verdict falls like a sheet of paper into the basket of life. Worn-out blood, you cried out, or almost. Breast cancer, that breast you never suckled because you had already come into this world, into another world, since your weight was fine despite the cold and privations. Fermented blood, still waiting for germination. Your mother's breasts were already sagging like a pair of wet washcloths when you nestled at her bosom for the first time: she was a middle-aged wide-hipped woman in her late forties, a lover of classical music and Somalian philology.

Vera Garvey remained quiet, stupefied and ashamed, before she trotted away, wiggling her little pantherlike ass. You threw some hard words in her face. Worn-out blood. Exhausting chemotherapy. What does she know of the inevitable decline, the duration of darkness, the race against the clock? Of Mama's reddened eyes, looking at no one? Of her lips chapped by fever, her ashen color, dull hair, chest choking in an animal sob? A sob that rises, grazes the peaks, and ricochets off the clarion stop of the Baptist cathedral's organ nearby. What does she know of the medicinal smell that permeates the whole house and prevents you and your father from sleeping?

You instinctively sharpen your system of self-defense, as you've always done. And you instantly left Vera Garvey. You run until you're breathless along the Edouard Glissant memorial. You keep running, you make yourself light and take off. You've become a stork from the foggy countries, from over there, where it seems you have family.

Now you are sailing into the gray of the northern sky, crossing the Mediterranean, gliding over Aquitaine, up toward the meadows of Normandy to build up your strength. Now you are a stork from the countries of sweltering heat. Not bound by any border. A bird of the roads of the sky, magnetized by flight, attracted by voyages, stops, intermittent and prodigious flights. A winged creature swallowed up by the impassable core of the night. Caught up by the quest for the flash of a meteor beyond the desert, the waves and whirlwinds of atoms. A figurehead at the prow refusing to dawdle at the stern.

Your mother was not yet your mother, and you were not you yet. You weren't even a clot of blood, not even a drop of sperm or a grain of sand, and not yet an atom of oxygen and hydrogen. You were nothing. A nonentity, an abstraction, a waiting horizon. You were nothing. Zero. Nada. *Rien.* "You've lost one love and the world is empty"[4]—or left only with phonies like your neighbor Vera Garvey. In other words, brain-dead people like Kwaku Osei, the CEO of Simba Records with his Ultrabright smile, the ex-tennis-champ Yannick Noah and your neighbors across the street, all obsessed by their diet, parking problems, or the surge in real estate prices. The world missed you but you didn't want to join the choir. You did not exist when Doctor Papa left to go abroad and during all those years he spent on Reunion Island, then in Mexico and from Mexico to Western Europe, continuing his venture as a doctor to the poor, attending to clinics in the hedges of Gironde, in Andalusia or the Carpathians, carrying all the misery of Manhattan on his back, running vaccination campaigns, helping to eradicate poliomyelitis (still raging in the malaria-ridden lagoon of Venice) while writing his doctoral thesis. He will finish out his career as doctor to the poor in one of those republics rich in syllables and bloody customs to the south of Russia.

Since when has this little old man, who is now rereading the same authors here before your eyes (Nuruddin Farah, Chinua Achebe, or Emmanuel Dongala, all winners of the prestigious Lalibela Prize),

4. Famous line from a poem by Alphonse de Lamartine (1790–1869): *Un seul être vous manque et tout est dépeuplé.*—Translators' note.

replaced the Good Samaritan who slogged over smugglers' trails from the Palatine Rhineland to Macedonia on his way to Galicia? When did he happen upon you? Or rather, when did you have the good fortune to happen upon him? To think that you have absolutely no memory of your life before that, when you were four! No matter how hard you try. Nothing but silhouettes, spots of color glimpsed through a fogged-up window. You imagine that your family's world was the size of the little patch of Norman greenery where you saw the light of day, a little patch of greenery shredding like a sweater that unravels with a pulled stitch. The banks of the Seine (was it the Seine, or the Orne or the Touques?) irrigated your blood, strengthened your bones. You are made out of their silt. But contrary to the saying "Happiness is in your own backyard," so popular and so untrue, it wasn't—not over there, anyway.

19 *In which we pass by all kinds of people on our street, both day and night.*

She's walking on all fours, advancing in fits and starts by the strength of her shoulders, dragging her hindquarters, raising a halo of dust visible from afar. The sun is at its height. Often she sinks her head back into her torso to catch her breath; then she stretches out her neck like a tortoise to set off once again. Every four or five steps she stops to wipe her brow, her face red from the strain, dripping with sweat. She closes her eyes reflexively, or to protect herself from pollution. Struggling along, she gains two steps. It's not hard to follow her, even hours later, for her knees are protected by two round pieces of Guelwar rubber; they leave two neatly parallel tracks, like a boat leaving behind an indelible souvenir in the form of a stream of oil in the calm water after it has left port. Dust is her natural element, not water, not fire, even in this part of the capital. Water and fire are synonyms for the twin girls who are accompanying her, or more precisely following her, around the Place de la Liberté. Their mischievous childish spirit keeps them there, on the lookout for a traffic accident, or holding out their hand to taxi drivers, or filching a banana from one of the Greek groceries of Fela-Anikulapo Kuti Boulevard. These two are capable of transforming a trivial rumor into a marvelous tale full of angels, archangels, genies, and *mamiwatas*.

Sometimes they're joined by another little devil named Ryszard, from central Poland, more precisely from Lowicz. He's capable of talking to you for hours on end without ever losing his excitement. Ryszard is scrawniness incarnate, an obsessive teller of tales. Poland is far away and no one here has an honest view of that inaccessible country, he claims between two bursts of laughter. He's one of the band of students who came to the United States to study in the left-wing universities of certain states from Lumumbashi to Ouagadougou or in a few theaters and dance companies buried in the savannah, toward Dar es Salaam. He has never lost his irrepressible urge to tell anyone who happens to cross his path about the charms of Krakow or the eternal snows of Gdansk, to open people's eyes to the untold wonders of Pomerania. Since nobody listens to him, his enthusiasm has eroded with time. His skin has hardened. He's become used to the asphalt, tamed it and adopted it along with the laws of the urban jungle and our contagious, planetwide values. In the street, he thrashes about like a maniac to occupy his piece of sidewalk. At the moment, Ryszard makes use of his talents as a petty thief and occasional storyteller in Soweto Park, two blocks from the Bank of Carthage.

The face of the lady who sells newspapers at her spot in front of the Bank of Carthage breaks out into a big smile. She recognizes you right away. Now she's dragging herself along on her backside as she smiles at you, a mere five yards costing her a mountain of superhuman efforts. She reaches your feet, you go forward to meet her. She sits up, slipping her dead legs under her laterite boubou, holding out today's paper as she does every Thursday around ten, when you go out to get a few little things downtown.

"Good Lord in heaven, if it isn't Maya! How you doin', sweetie?"

You say nothing. Her face tenses up. The old pain lodged at the bottom of her backbone tells her it's still there. It spreads first to the spine, then throughout her body. The old familiar pain is back. It isn't about to let go. It's in the air the old woman is breathing, it swathes her with all its force, all its evil power. It can neither leave her nor conquer her. The city is humming all over, the old pain is isolating Mariette the cripple. You can't share your pain with others, not even with the fruit of your womb.

Annette and Lucette, the twins that follow her around everywhere, don't know anything about it, and it's not their fault. All three of them have the mark of abuse on their brow. They've come from God knows where—refugees from Tbilisi, Winnipeg, or more likely, Normandy. They have crossed dozens of countries. They were so undernourished their hair turned orange. Ever since their arrival on African soil, it's mum's the word and keep your mouth shut. The big questions with no immediate answers? Abandoned. The burning questions, like who they were and why they were what they were, forgotten. You'll learn later they were born in a little Norman village in the midst of uncouth farmers. But the war against the Bretons, their intimate enemies, regularly ravaged that cursed country. Any reason was good enough to go on the warpath: the status of Mont Saint-Michel, the division of wells and pastures, the competition between belfries or the conflict over sardine fishing. The militiamen told them: "You're lucky, you have two choices: flight, or the grave. The others only had the second choice." That's how they left, empty-handed, without so much as a needle in their pockets or a shawl on their shoulders. It took them six months to reach this country and eight more to get here, in front of this bank, in the middle of this crowd that bows down only to the greenback, the precious guinea that enables them to gulp down McDiops by the ton and hectoliters of Safari beer.

One day a beggar saw you and whispered in old Mariette's ear: "Where's that girl from? She ain't like the other ones. Her skin's white like limestone." And Mariette made a face, her disapproving grin meaning "She's her mother's daughter" before answering calmly: "Hey, she's a daughter of Adam and Eve, like everybody else in this world." Good for you, Mariette!

You ran away from him. You caught your breath between the Bank of Carthage and Ifrikiya's crafts shop, you ran the rest of the way at top speed. Doctor Papa was waiting for you, or rather calling you from afar. You knew it, you could feel it.

20 *In which we tell of a strange people of the night whose fate is not to be envied. Nay, not one jot!*

"We by night

If the sea turned into ink, it would not exhaust all our dreams, our words, our stammering, our reiterations, our pages to read-write, our future books of wind, in the same second, the same fever, the same breath. All the desires of our blood, all the will to live of our guts, all the clandestine passion of our words. Our words well up from the deepest night, a black night, but black bottomless blue-black, with no rhyme or reason. A night violating all the mornings of the world, all the mornings of life, yours as well as ours. A night no different from the sun that skins you, detaches retinas, throws out blackish flames, drags around live embers, firebrands fed by pure oxygen, vigorous fires, cyclones of acetylene followed by floods of ash for days and nights all mingled together. Thus it is night and what about the skies lit a giorno for all eternity? What about our drifts, peregrinations, divagations, hallucinations? Maelstroms of zephyrs and trade winds corrupting the lava flows driven to the Baltic Sea and even to that damn Mediterranean separating us from you and your fat, well-fed Africa, belching with comfort and boredom. Ah, that great overfed Africa will soon be something for our teeth and claws! Yum, yum! Yes, us, clustered on the cliffs, caves, ridges, dunes, rocks and backwash of the opposite shore. Us, stuck to its walls like an oyster to a rock, like hot air balloons prevented from taking off. Us enough of it all, sick of it all, fed up to here, fed up to our asses, basta and amen to stewing in the Cayenne pepper of hunger and thirst . . . Us, wanting and desiring, and begging to drink, eat, be nourished, live, urinate, defecate, belch, and even bathe in the blood of the industrial slaughterhouses of fat Africa, devoted to fitness and facelifts. Us, wanting to cross open spaces, mountains, oceans, inland seas, straits, estuaries, wanting to go through doubts, loneliness, mourning, and sadness. Us, up from afar, from the Ardennes, the Urals, Bohemia, the Black Forest, Cornwall, and every famine. Us, called chain-gang bandits, castaways from Gibraltar, drowned-saved from Tunisian beaches, survivors of old tubs sailing under Liberian or Filipino flags, sunk and escaped from Albanian smugglers, stateless, claiming to be Kurds, enlisted-rejected as Bosnian, Ukrainian, children of the Bosporus born in the crevasse between feverish Europe and misty Asia, refugees surrounded by their bags and brats. As we wait for them to be killed, all of us must rise above our own imprisonment through the great escape of the word, through the calligraphy of our dreams, through poetry, so we can say everything, spit out everything, write everything. Everything. Us, wanting to be cheek and jowl with the well fed, well housed, well off: mouth-to-mouth with all those snotty girls, a good heart-to-heart with all those bored old guys chafing in the hospices of death from Asmara to Praia. Us, giving you heart after your heart, cancer, gullet, chest operation. A brand new heart for all the bachelors, single women, all the mateless souls—all the broken hearts up for grabs, standing, sitting or lying down. Us, trumpeting, raging, fulminating, bursting with health and utopias, ready for daring hand-to-hand combat with athletes, dancers, rope or trapeze jumpers, foot, car, or bike racers. All that for free. Us not far off, soon to appear in your country. Us, already at your door, at your barricades, your fences, your cinderblock walls. You, already huddling inside your cities, stations, airports, parks, with the sound of apocalypse ahead of our every step. Us, wetbacks, split-heads, white skin-and-bones, mangy dogs, poisonous turtles, irascible billy goats, motherless little rats, salt thieves, pallid gypsies, ashen zombies, and a whole tankful of curses as yet unheard . . . Ah, if the sea could turn into ink, we could name and find the flavor and value of every insult you throw in our faces, at our heads, and our backs too."

These words from beyond the grave come from a letter the Coast Guard found in the pocket of a potential exile lying on the beach of Port Sudan. He must have been a fine writer, a poet or philosopher, a thousand miles away from the stereotype of the naked immigrant, savage and fierce. His abrasive language and unbridled style unquestionably attest to this fact. These hammering, clashing words, spread through the Web by an antiglobalization site well known to activists (http://www.restorehope.org), have moved many citizens of the first continent. You can bet that poet's dead and gone!

TWO   *A Voyage to the Heart of the Studio*

21

In which your humble servant sketches the true portrait of the artist as a young girl full of talent—and insolent, to take the cake.

The tight framing of the famous painting by Gustavio Mbembe sends you back to your present inclinations, to your inner flame, to the natural bent of your desires, am I wrong, Maya? And you dared to confess it to your parents. You really are incorrigible. What cheek! That work of art is to good taste what unkempt hair is to combed, what an empty theater is to a crowded forum or a cudgel is to a Kampala canoness. The subject is only a piece of flesh, according to the clinical words of Mbembe himself, in other words "the belly and reddish-brown sex of a woman with her thighs spread apart and her torso thrown back." That girl's ass is more beautiful and intelligent than lots of faces, you think slyly. Asmara shows the same hypocrisy as the other capitals of the South made rich by the postindustrial revolution. Sex is both taboo and an object of fascination. But what really aroused your ever-present curiosity was the amazing destiny of the painting, the crazes it aroused, its appearances and disappearances, its jumble of voyages.

Its adventurous fate is worthy of the hero of a novel. First given to its sponsor, Khalil Bey, the Ottoman ambassador at Addis Ababa, grand vizier and great gambler before God, it went from hand to hand, from era to era, from fat Africa to the banks of the Bosporus, and then from the Danube to cachectic Hungary, and finally from the Nazis to the Soviets before ending up in the country home of a little pimp named Jacques Lacan. Remember, Malaïka, he hid it behind an abstract painting, whisking the smoldering beauty of Gustavio Mbembe's inaugural scene away from eager eyes. A painting of this quality is more than a painting, it's a place to go, an inhabited space. A taste to be shared. Protected by a thick pane of glass, *The Origin of the World* was finally admired for a few weeks in the Mongo Beti Museum in Massawa, which had paid a small fortune to acquire it.

Everything has gone back to normal in this affair, as it did twenty years ago with the world-famous smile of the Mouna Sylla, stolen by a Caucasian from a Tuscan hamlet named Florence. Gustavio Mbembe's masterpiece is preserved in the holy of holies, the African Humanity Museum (AHM) in the federal capital, and watched over day and night by four guards equipped with state-of-the-art technology.

For you, emotion is a jewel. Nature is a chaos that must be ordered, a task that belongs to artists. "An absurd undertaking," was Doctor Papa's diagnosis. "An attractive fantasy that would never even occur to a regular fellow," your mother continued, suddenly struck with anxiety, your mother who was first kora of the Martin Luther King orchestra of Mogadishu in her early youth. A fantasy she hoped would pass. But you don't see it that way. You buckle down to work, you work yourself to death and that's all there is to it. You move away from reality, which strikes a pose and imposes its diktats. With whatever is available, that is, with your nerves, muscles, and moods, you get down to the grind. From the land of your dreams you quickly brought back a lovely little painting with an evocative title, *Inner Chaos*, which sums up your inspiring project perfectly; eternally reworked, it is worthy of Sisyphus. Far from incantation and praise. And it is no surprise that standing in front of your garden, or more exactly your studio, we face a new world. A world of reverie, imagination, fiction. An amazing space where stars, suns, skies, and planets fuse in a joyful confusion. Vaults of soap bubbles rise, iridescent and ephemeral. The hum and turbulence of the world are mixed with the gold of its sands.

That isn't all. You have more than enough physical resources. All you have to do, Malaïka, is cut across dunes, walk, stop, breathe, in order to draw or write. Words, images, sentences rise up in you, take hold of your hand and take shape as stones, a snake, a crescent moon bright as a lemon, low walls and silhouettes. Space and time—everything—in a great embrace. Everything ablaze. Sap bubbles up, traces delicate pathways. People and places are mixed in a whirlwind of reflections, waves and moving shadows. Instants breathe eternity. You can exchange pure words with fish in the stream. You take delight in a bowl of white rice enhanced with bits of Nile perch, a handful of hazelnuts and a pitcher of white Abunawas wine. After your belly, you must feed your muscles. Ah, you love to run, Maya. To fly away at top speed as if you were riding a Tartar thoroughbred. The trade winds, the monsoon, sea currents, and the khamsin carry you off to a world like none other. You are the wandering monk seeking grace. The hermit of the mountains and flowers who has chosen a solitary retreat. You lend an ear to the slightest murmur. You contemplate nothingness—while lemon trees, camellias, branches of wild olive trees protect you from the assaults of the sun. How long till the next blossoming?

That isn't all. You have tremendous admiration for Gerard Sekoto, Skunder Boghossian, and their tropicalist friends, Maya. Sekoto and his colorful, bidimensional, haughty works have a place of choice in the shows of your personal museum. In the midpoint of your adolescence you also contracted a huge debt to Wifredo Lam and the Gorean school. You are well aware of all that. Very early on, you left the path that others had laid out for you. To each his arm of the sea to row, you reflect. Your route is never straight, your sidesteps are legion. You measure life with the yardstick of a bird's-eye view. You find it tedious to concoct menus or programs; you'd rather trust chance. Lady luck smiled on you: there you are, studying under several masters on the West Coast—hence your solid technique in sculpture. Recently, in the state of Niger, more precisely in Zinder, you did a series of studies with a magnificent green palette that revealed the green landscapes of this trans-Saharian countryside, like the Horn of Africa where you grew up.

That isn't all. The critics did not turn up their noses at your work. Quite the contrary, the shock they got has never stopped shaking them up. I remember that one of them—I think it was Babefemi Babalawo—pointed out that your busts have the advantage of setting the instantaneous emotion of the viewer into immutable stone. He compared your work to the energy and daring of a John Coltrane. And even your early works will not go unnoticed in our region, this land of stone and clay where the hieratic palm trees watch over meadows of grain like the sun over the Earth. There's no doubt you spontaneously found your style there, since your creations dialogue with this land. It sometimes looks like it could yield paintings in the genre of the Grand Palais (ah, its heavy chandeliers, its gilded ceiling!) or the enchantments of the MAAMM, the Museum of African Art of Maputo in Mozambique; and sometimes sculptures in the style of the bare Ahaggar mountains, the cliffs of Gondar, the tree trunks tightroping over the sand ergs. There is no doubt about it: you create a sensorial commerce between this territory and the rest of the world. Such an event is rarely repeated and you know it.

Art requires work and sweat, the desire not to please right away. Or worse, at any price. So true art is the opposite of demagogy or kitsch: according to the scholarly article of Amiri Baraka in the *Africana Encyclopedia*, kitsch "reveals the attitude of someone who wants to please the greatest number at any price." You try to show patience, be demanding and not let your tension fall, for sculpture demands consistency and courage as high as Mount Cameroon. First you have to find a model, create complicity with that model, then do some hands-on work (Ah, your loving potter's hands! Your hands running along my skin, going down my back! I'm getting carried away, dear Maya). Chisel, refine, let it rest, dry, bake . . . and cast it all in bronze. That's how you go from the fingers of the artist to the marble of eternity. A rare privilege, isn't it? And yet, your sculptures do not look like anything we know here. And with good reason: shepherds like us, who have become very rich by the grace of God, have never cultivated the art of statuary: it was thought to be blasphemous, or limited to sedentary, agricultural peoples like the Dogons, the Yorubas, the Makondes and other ingenious peoples like the Balubas.

That isn't all. Some of your sculptures have delicate scars on their face that attract attention, as in *The Little Saint of Fouta-Djalon* (terracotta no. 21), whose hair is so wavy it looks like a bouquet of seaweed. Everywhere in the world, she will be recognized as a little Carmen from eternal Africa. Her little black and brown sisters in the brush are playing in the dust, on the hard-packed ground (*Nedjma and Amandla,* terracotta no. 4), writing the essential word together: "Freedom." This parable of the quest to surpass oneself and attain enlightenment is a piece of testimony, a thundering song for oppressed peoples, particularly in Ontario. Lines by the poet and novelist Alan Bacon (1903–1988), author of the famous novel *Cry The Beloved Province* (1978), fill out the scene with the first measures of the new national anthem: "*Free Canada! Oh My Lord, Free Canada Now!*"[5] The *Trois-Rivières Massacre* (terracotta no. 3) shows a violent scene, tragic in its intimacy. Elsewhere, a young woman, clearly Norwegian, is holding her dying child in her arms. Still elsewhere volunteer nurses armed with ladles stuff the gullets of little Maltese, Welsh, or Estonian children. It is easy to see how the most burning current events feed your daily work.

More intimist, *The Dove* (no. 7) or *The Pillow* (no. 8) seem to evoke personal crises. Solitude or nostalgia for the first figurine: a girl with a long cape thrown over her frail shoulders presses a white dove to her breast with infinite tenderness. An escapee from Noah's Ark, the bird symbolizes love and constancy, as everyone knows. Abandonment or perhaps weariness for the second figurine. In a much happier vein, *Aïda* (burnt sienna relief no. 26), a young Moldavian woman encountered in Mogadishu, radiates with life. Lively lines, solid colors.

Pieces like *Aïda, The Dancer* (no. 2) or *Ghosts* (no. 25) were baked twice. First browned in an electric oven to make them firm, and then plunged into water before being put back into a traditional brick wood-burning oven. When they are taken out they instantly change color from contact with the air.

Finally, you were incredibly good at embodying your environment, its taciturn men and women, while turning your back on the clean, pretty cities our architects have the knack of building: the artist is the guardian of the future, not the past. Better still, you succeeded

5. In English in the original.—Translators' note.

in inscribing them into clay, stone, and bronze for centuries and centuries to come. For example, that calm sailor, sitting facing the sea on the road to Tadjoura (*Contemplation*, no. 6), his eyes level with the horizon. It's a safe bet that our African Gods, with Shango in the lead, will help you stick to this path with the same ease and seriousness. No doubt you will inspire artistic vocations among the youngest of our immigrants.

22

*Now we are with Maya, who is caught in
the toils of love. How will she manage?
Our heart bleeds for her—as does Adama's.*

"Maya, my love, what are you saying?

*I am coming to life, and now I am facing your eyes of clay. I am coming to
life, and now I am outside the family forge. We are twins, united for life.
I am iron, you are flesh. We will be joined forever, skin against skin. You
will strut with me, I will be your eye of sun, your igneous part. I am knife
and dagger and lance, a male weapon in quest of a hoe, the female tool
that scratches and wounds and opens the womb of the Earth as my penis
will work your own womb to sow it. I am your twin brother, you are my
sister, my soul that I have found again. We came from the same bicephalous
fetus immediately buried under the great hoary baobab. I am made out of
you and vice versa. A strand of your hair is mixed with the brass wire that
crimps my trunk. In our country, we are born swords, daggers, jet knives,
harpoons, shields, hoes, or ceremonial sabers.*

*Maya, you will brandish me as dagger or lance or assegai. You know,
my love, I have no right to shed blood, to soil the forge, mother of all met-
als. I will follow you in your perpetual rotation on Earth. I will be your
shadow. Don't say anything, perhaps you will die before me. I will outlive
you, I will continue your life with the breath of your flesh and the bronze
of my breath. I will not grow old, I will keep the features of yesteryear in the
thick night of existence. I will watch over you like the oil-soaked wick that
resists the surrounding darkness. Your poem will come to me. The lines of
your hair, your clothes, the gleam of your eyes, the oval of your face with
its high cheekbones will be read on my chest. I will honor your life among
the living, we will be more than twins, forever. With the procession of the
years we will take on the rank of ancestors.*

You and I are as old as the night, the Iron Age, the age of the sacred wood. I am the son of live embers, the son of ashes hot as a human heart. You are human clay thrown on a potter's wheel by an agile-fingered God. You curve like a crescent moon. I am straighter than the iroko or the acoma tree. And what about my breath, my song in the lazy wind, the chants of my throat, the dance of my pearls, my tousled mane, and the eagle feathers I gird myself with on parade days! And what about my colors: blue like indigo dye as soon as the evening shows its muzzle, brown like a bad dream on a moonless night, flame when the beetle Sun lends me his jewels, straw when the clouds gather in a rug, emerald when the forest shelters me from the rain! Maya my love, you know all that. Not just the royal guinea hen, not just the Nile ibis; even the slightest goat kid knows it instinctively. The smallest waterfowl flying from stone to stone can feel it from afar. Maya, what are you saying? Why this silence? I await a word from you, a sigh."

You read and reread this declaration of love from Adama Traoré, the impatient suitor, the young artist and photographer you met in Accra Art School. You made each other's acquaintance in the very first days, in the lobby of this fine freestone edifice, encouraged by the great artists whose names are carved on the opal façade of the Institute. Very quickly you became friends. With no family ties in Accra, you made up a little clan of two, a phalanstery dedicated to the arts. This burning letter is not the first one he sent you since you broke up. More than a declaration of love, it is a pledge sworn between colleagues, friends of the forge and masters of fire. Together you had shared meals and passion. You had spent whole nights remaking the world. Your four hands together had crushed dangerous metallic oxides (the blue of cobalt, the yellow of manganese, the green of chrome and copper) to extract colors lively and light as a flock of hummingbirds. You are more than a little proud of this letter, Maya! It's obvious, even if you claim you don't have any time for love at the moment.

23

But Adama is not the only one sending her passionate missives, far from it. And our heroine's creations repel the agents of the spirit of evil, who are akin to demons.

"Malaïka's Visual Poems

A traveler in quest of an artistic ideal, a perpetual nomad bivouacking in the wake of her roving parents, Malaïka succeeded—at least psychologically—in laying out her notebook, pencils, hollow reeds, and charcoal crayons and setting up her easel wherever she went for the past few years. From Namibia to Djibouti, from Cap Verde to Toamasina, Kinshasa to Bobo-Dioulasso, where she had drawn a breath of fresh air at the side of an old, wise writer, and then to the end of the night of Mitteleuropa, which is at the heart of her latest work—a focal place if ever there was one, because it still keeps the memory of the genocide of the Jews intact.

This recent highly spiritual work fits into the scheme of the quest referred to above. In it, one feels the pulse of the threads woven from yesterday to today, one perceives something like faith emerging, even if God is strikingly absent from this work. The artist probably did not resist the appeal of such an exciting and demanding situation for long (Shoah, The Last Butterfly). Again she takes up the motif of the innocent body, manhandled, disfigured and twisted in every direction before it is finally reduced to dust in the camps of Auschwitz, Birkenau, or Terezina. We have recently seen the wing of this same madness, this same barbarity, brush against our doors.

The artist has kept intact the soul of her childhood. Give a ball of clay to a child and he'll invent a fantastic bestiary. What is more, she does her best to explore the visible sooty traces, clearly etched in our collective consciousness haunted by the Holocaust, to feel them with her fingers. She has been able to breathe hope, vigor and new life into this great sick body. And as *she did this, she caressed it, cosseted it for a long time. She has brought it back to life, since she called it* Survival.

Of all the plastic arts, sculpture is the one that goes furthest in the imitation of divine creation. At the beginning was the emotion embodied in clay. At the beginning was the gesture of the hand, two small steps before the coming of the Word. Since then, according to the African legend, God or Mother Nature has sowed in this vast world—and not only in a few cursed spots like the canyons of Colorado or wealthy places like the Saharan Tassili or the mysterious Easter Island—visual poems capable of moving the most insensitive among us. Sculpture captures the instant and fixes it for eternity. It freezes the sap of palpitating life, ends movement, dispersion, and evaporation to set it in another time, another life. A life turned into stone. Petrifaction pleasing to the eye. Sudden paralysis of contained forces, of packed muscles, of limbs now imposing as in our great Ousmane Sow, now threadlike as the burning silhouettes of Djiatto Mehdi (1901–1966) that remind us of so many nomads on the line of the horizon. We are called upon to recognize the plurality of the world in its representations, its languages, its primal gestures, and also in its ashes. Transfigured by the artist's work, the shadows of the past awake, opening to the sun. After all, we are only passing through on this Earth, we are not born with knowledge. That's why we still need stories, fables, myths, and always will (the Golem from Jewish folklore is the main theme in this series) and cosmogonies. The poetic fable of Ntoni Bizimana (The Butterfly) *tells us the same thing. If the ending is terrible, it is because the poet is sending us, above and beyond our condition of poor mortals, back to the impossible dialogue between beauty* (The Liberated Butterfly) *and unspeakable barbarity* (The Ghetto.)

    Without the God of Genesis, without Adam, we know that the Golem would only be a mute, shapeless giant. In the same way, before casting it in bronze, Malaïka kneads the clay to allow the little girl with the butterfly to rise, thus repeating the immemorial gesture of the magician described in the Kabbalah. It was not rare for a Golem to take the form of an animal, a lion, a tiger or a snake . . . Here, the butterfly accompanies the child in the artist's desire for elevation. We know that the butterfly represents—Holy Writ attests to it—the soul freed from its fleshly yoke and bitter saliva, the soul in search of divine wine, the soul burning with mystic love. Another aspect of this symbolism alludes to metamorphosis and anamorphosis. The chrysalis as the potentiality of being, the butterfly as the symbol of resurrection. All that is palpable in Malaïka's sculpture, which here manages to become a kind of exhumation, a work of mourning. She has bequeathed these essential works to our fragile human condition. We thank her with all our humility and all the force of our admiration."

Kwame Appiah, *Revue noire* no. 49, Éditions du Papyrus, Musée des Arts nègres, Dakar, pp. 130–134.

24 *In which we tell of our heroine's voyage to Ghana. Her return and the torments of her soul.*

When you graduated from the Accra Art School, you went right back to your home state on the East Coast, at least four time zones and thirteen hours away by plane. Your mother was slowly dying, the fax you picked up at the Kotoka airport at a cybercafé squeezed between a Tanganyika Steak House and a Chimurenga Café told you nothing new. You put your head between your shoulders and went back to your old hangdog look. You cried silently during the whole flight.

No more walks along the port and its warehouses, its refinery oil tanks, industrial wastelands, perpetual construction sites. Gone were its beautiful cranes, bulk carriers, tankers, and drydocks. Vanished, the colorful silhouettes, the Ashanti charm, the peaceful backcountry landscape now ruined by real estate speculation. In Accra, in Kumasi and elsewhere, they took apart the factories they thought were unproductive. They razed neighborhoods and cities to build nice apartments, expensive condos, and huge shopping malls. The people modernity ditched along the way and trampled on were told to pack up and leave. The immigrants too.

Just before you left, you were down for some time. You were all wrinkled pants, restless sleep, frozen food, and cramps. Your psychological health was really worrisome, Maya. Then you perked up. Your taste for creation returned, you climbed out of the bottomless pit you had sunk into to rediscover the blue of the doors, shutters, and sky of the Côte d'Or. When you return to Asmara, you immediately hunt out similarly inspiring landscapes near Hargheisa in the neighboring state of Somaliland. You won't be missing the gay, anarchic atmosphere of your three years at art school as much—your hands in paint, drippings, rust, and mold. You're not the type to stay put in dusty rooms and trace perspectives and vaults with a square. What you love above all is to knead matter wherever it may come from, to run your hand over peeling façades, to feel in the palm of your hand the halos of humidity ochering the walls and scratch off strips of wallpaper with your nails.

Between observing and diving into something there is an intimidating distance that many students refuse to cross, you would have pointed out to Doctor Papa if he hadn't been pacing up and down in a deserted corridor of Alioune Diop Hospital at that very moment. As always, Maya, you're attracted by everything that embraces life. You don't ask yourself questions. Oh, no! You act—instinctively. You drive away morbid ideas by projecting yourself into daydreams with powerful esthetic images. You try to inhabit the object of your creation. You are subjugated by the exhilaration of chance, which turns a patch of wall or ground into abstract paintings through the play of light or some other intervention. You admire what is right there, what happens all by itself. Since you're superstitious, you don't tell anyone about it before the work is done, contrary to some of your classmates who elaborate theoretical discourses before applying a single brushstroke to canvas. They leave their paint jars to lecture with incredible chutzpah. They quote art critics like Seyoum Kiflé, Okwui Enwezor, and Olu Guibe, Makonnen-era philosophers or today's video artists. Stock phrases fly from their mouths like eagle feathers, or fall like dead leaves. Many's the time you've heard them chewing over expressions like "clear line," "rhythmic motor," "existential emptiness," "death of the author," "the catalepsy of African art," or "the shifting of tints à la so-and-so." You wonder where they get all these ideas from. "Ah, my friends, what nonsense!" Doctor Papa would normally have retorted, hugging you tenderly at the airport.

This habit of storing up masses of images goes back to your childhood. Everything that fell into your hands would be put away, carefully deposited in your boxes and canvas bags full of discards. Family photos, holy images of the *gnawa* religion, postcards of wild animals, labels from cans, florist catalogues, advertising brochures, scraps of paper picked up from the street, soiled with footprints. Later, you will go from discovery to discovery, from wonder to wonder. Your use of techniques as varied as photography, engraving, and lithography dazzled your teachers. You keep repeating that creation is ninety-nine percent perspiration and one percent inspiration, an obvious truth worth remembering once and for all. You also think you understand that art is not an end in itself, just the way to express the incredible vitality that has always inhabited you. No need to become the darling of the Johannesburg gallery owners and the avant-gardists from the west coast of Guinea Bissau to Tunis in order to enjoy each moment of life. No desire at all to be included in the network of contemporary art. Life first, career second, that is your credo. Doctor Papa would have silently approved of you as he picked up your little bag.

You get home in a taxi. Everything is quiet. Your true mother is gone. Her body is still at the morgue. Tomorrow, everything will be over. The tears, the prayers, the funeral. After forty days of mourning, you'll take charge of Doctor Papa's daily life. There is a life after death, you tell yourself. And life must go on here and now.

In which the games of love and chance take center stage. A songwriter puts in his two cents' worth.

For Adama, you are a dream incarnate, a pure fantasy, a rare beauty—a cross between an ingénue, a temptress, and a child-woman—and you know it. You take advantage of that even if you refuse to admit it. Never in a month of African Sundays will you answer. It would be simpler to just tell him yes or no. You can also tell him "Be patient" or "Life is elsewhere, without me." But you worry yourself sick, obsessed as you are by your own story. Who was your father? And your mother? One ought to speak of procreators rather than parents here. What presided over your birth? Why you? Why? How? Who? What? You keep unwinding the same rosary of anxiety.

Meanwhile Adama is brooding; he writes you passionate letters you leave unanswered. You find him as useless as the king in an incomplete deck of cards. You cling to reality. You put aside fine sentiments in favor of daily life. That's how you take off, with the ball at your foot, heading for the goal across the field, burning to kick life into the net without weakness or hesitation. Poor Adama has no idea to what extent you can be a monster of selfishness. "What's wrong with loving you, writing you, setting down a bit of madness on the burning paper of my heart? What's wrong with worrying myself blue, with gathering illusions? Answer me," he begs, with his letters for intermediaries. He would rather let himself be hacked into pieces by the little tyrants of Saudi Arabia than suffer your silence, which he takes for scorn. He persists, stubbornly: "I beg you, tell me something that will lift me up into the dangerous heights of dreams, into the silky cashmere of heaven."

Your only reply is to raise your eyebrows. But he is relentless. And you confine him to the closets of forgetting. And he cries his eyes out, pursuing the white whale of his madness. And you take refuge in silence. And he summons all the poets, all the griots of Africa. And you play dead. And he bangs on the closed door with the dramatic bangs of mad love. And you let him soliloquize, you who think life is a breeze, a well-oiled mast you can climb up and shinny down as many times as you have to. You who maintain that real life is a trickle of water between the banks of the womb and the banks of the grave. You should come down to Earth, Maya, forget your mischievous pride for a moment and remember the advice of Robert Marley. Tell yourself *Wake up and live now!* Instead of contemplating your navel while wondering what he sees in you, for deep down you see yourself as a hollow oyster, invisible. Invisible is truly the right word. Often, you see yourself as invisible. Yes, you have no shadow, no picture of yourself. You are also absent from your own dreams. You really are invisible, there's no doubt about it. It happens at night, when you take your clothes off before going to bed: you look at yourself in the mirror and you can't see a thing.

Who does Adama Traoré want to catch in the lasso of his love? Is it you, who don't exist in your own eyes? Your ghost, or the girl who's an artist, painter, and sculptress to boot?

26 *All the flowers and all the poisons in the world come to meet in the garden of our taciturn heroine.*

Everything happens at night. And late at night, when the firmament is fringed with trails of brilliant dust, is when you work in the glass-roofed studio at the back of the garden, perfumed with kerosene and swarming with insects. It's the meeting place of small reptiles, crickets, grasshoppers, praying mantises, bunches of bats, blind geckos, and gray lizards in heat. This is where you knead clay. Once Doctor Papa has gone to sleep, knocked out by herbal teas and his medication (when he has denied himself a glass of a robust Stellenbosch or a fruity Abunawas from a good year), you get busy on your own. From a neighboring dune rich in Euphorbiaceae, you take the silt you need for your clay pies, which will keep their laterite color or take on a new one from various additives, depending. You manage to make your figurines rise. You could almost compete with the female potters of Swaziland who flood the whole world with their cheap mass-produced creations! Come on, Maya, relax! I'm kidding.

For you, it's still almost an innocent game, a virus you caught when you were a little girl. The activity of an only child to channel her excess energy. You etch exotic motifs on your figurines, or sometimes you paint them on. In their brilliant attire, they look exactly like the totems we inherited from ancient peoples. They emerge from the whitewaters of mirage and speak to us of the origins and legends of bygone days. They are born from almost nothing, from a whim. From a dream or a murmur. You work terribly hard at making your laterite dolls incarnate the genies of the sands, hiding behind the next dune and lying in wait for the lost traveler. Because you are and will always be one of those restless souls for whom the world of appearances is not enough. You do your utmost to delve deep into everything, to the bone, to the nerve. Even as a child, you would remain aloof from the arguments everybody ordinarily gets dragged into. You are waiting for better times to come, you are waiting for the joyful evening wind.

Only birds manage to live by their quills, not men, who lack feathers, and certainly not artists who turn candle ends and bits of string into honey. What price can we put on the eye of someone like Cameron Quenum, whose paintings come as close as possible to piercing the mystery of life, his vision anchored at the root of things, mixing the most intimate details in order to burn them in the sacred fire of his imagination? What could possibly be traded for the thundering voice of the voodoo priest Papa Legba or the compassionate magic of Rabbi Chaim Melki, marveling over the tiniest creature, taking it in his arms, stroking it as he strides ahead, making the stone floor ring under the steps of his light boots. You have always been on the side of the poor, the madman, the angel, the child, the stammerer, the pariah, and the stranger wearing stripes. A voracious observer, anything is grist for your mill, and you suck your nectar from every flower under the sun.

All kinds of pots, basins, buckets with or without a handle, trowels, spatulas, scrapers, chipped gourds are lying around the garden. The watering cans are stored in the back, facing what used to be the little shack, painted and repainted every year, where you used to play with your neighbors and passing cousins. That's where you must have learned to play house with one of those little rascals and discovered the private topography of your body. And there, in the back of that garden of the senses, in those moments of games and innocence, you discovered the unforgettable, the undeniable: no, Maya, you were not like other people!

Your skin was white as milk. Pale as an albino. You had hidden this obvious fact from yourself for a long time. There's no use putting on elves' boots, there are things you can never get away from. A new alphabet dawned before your eyes that afternoon, when you discovered your difference. You set your first words to paper. Words of anger, shouting about that injustice. Words of anguish, of panic. Howled words, a thousand miles from the frozen speech of adults. From now on you will be burned by the mystery of your origins, the slow growth of your troubling body, the almost tactile approach of death. You immediately felt estranged from yourself. And you became asthmatic for the rest of your life.

You also made new resolutions. No more games in the shack. Away with the little scoundrels. From then on, you would play by yourself. And you'll look for a sign, a wink, a little droplet of explanation in your parents' eyes. Never again will you be happy like babies with their thumbs. Later, at the mere memory of that afternoon in the shack, your body will stiffen, your ears will close. You will watch every gesture you make, every step you take. As soon as you hear children shouting in the street, you'll shut yourself up in your room and you'll dive into a book. A few days later, the first insults will fly at you on the way to school. "Foreign-face," "Milk-face," "Curd-face" . . . and why not skull-face, you protested the first time. Nothing will ever discourage your little enemies. They kept on chanting "Milk-skin," "Sour-milk skin" as soon as they came up to you or cornered you in front of the door of the Ahmadou Kourouma elementary school. Often, you'll run away before the worm-eaten hulk of the door collapses on you. "Milk-face": that was the most indelible insult thrown out by those cow-brained kids, an insult that burned like lime because you had never paid any attention to the color of your skin. You had repressed that aspect of your person. You had identified so completely with your parents and the people around you that you would launch into Claude Nougaro's song without the slightest ironic distance: *Armstrong, I'm not black. My skin is white.*

All the flowers and all the poisons in the world come to meet in your garden. When you can see the sun sinking into the sea at the end of the highway and its halo turning the suburbs pink, it's time to sit on the porch and listen to the sap zigzagging through the tree trunks, the lisping of the dragonflies, the moon about to break into a big grin, the swarming of the twilight and its sheet of coolness, the owls hooting from the tops of the mango trees, the soft swishing of the artificial river out there at the end of the highway, and the bear cubs on the other side of the Mediterranean, in the Northern Hemisphere, stricken with cold and famine, roaming from den to den: from the mother bear's den to the neighbors' den, from the neighbors' to the assembled cousins' den, and from there to the home of the patriarch with white streaks of hair. These cubs are so gentle that bears like to rub down their skin with an oily salve, stroke their downy sides, tickle and pet them—a long, complex ceremony magnificently orchestrated by the bears' grandmother. After which, the cubs have the right to live like adults: raise families, steal food from the hairy men whose dearest dream is bear stew with honey, challenge competitors to a duel, inform the tribe of the arrival of a rainbow over there, far away, where the sky has given birth to a sperm-colored mountain.

27 *"Where will we go tomorrow, we whose desires are without end?" asked, long ago, one of our African poets who had the laugh of an archangel. Adama's travels are as much a sensual quest as a historical and geographical exploration.*

Adama Traoré is a fashion photographer in everyday life, a sculptor in the secret safe of his heart. In the past, his sharp eyes had roamed the globe, watching blood flowing in the Balkans, tracking columns of refugees from Siberia to Alaska. Now his eyes caress the lavishness of Monomotapa and the theme parks of Tipaza, when he's not fixing girls' legs on glossy paper. From now on, his little black case (Maïga brand) is now dancing to the rhythm of Brazilian *batucadas* or the rumbas of Zaïko Langa Langa.

Clearly Adama Traoré's family history bears the stamp of our colonial past, so often passed over in silence. A gap that spoils the feast of the intelligence, sapping from inside the communities our ancestors destroyed throughout these last centuries. Everything began with a name, a family gift stored in memory left untilled. You probably don't know that the Traorés were a patrician family, Maya, at times colonizers out of bravado, unlike people like the Mwangis, Sisulus, Secks, Belingas, and Ratsimonias who squeezed the juice out of Europe and North America from the year 1596 on.

This conquest smells of gunpowder from afar. It has made a black niche for itself in the national imagination; it has the force of a hurricane. One can detect it as readily in the people's saliva as in the spluttering of the academics of today and yesterday. A bit more than four centuries later, we try to celebrate this historic date with panache. Paltry conquerors like the Traorés wouldn't have pounced on the white cake with the rage of men whose lives were intimately linked to raids and plunder. In the country of Emperor Makonnen, the invaders were kings; they always took to the sea, as in the historical epic films of Youssef Chahine. Thus in 1792, at the order of Tewodros, son of Makonnen, two hundred and seventy one thousand men and twenty-six vehicles made of solid wood charged up the steep winding roads over Belgrade, the idea being to push in ahead of the Turkish pashas who ruled over the eastern front of Europe.

Post-Makonnian madness was not lacking in violence or intelligence. As it went along, it built the longest funicular railway in the world (eighty-four kilometers), which was then taken down and stolen by the same Turks who lived side by side with Adama's ancestors. It had all the energy and ambition necessary to do the job. It is responsible for laying down roads, digging tunnels, building bridges and the Montenegro railroad (inaugurated in 1911), and for the memories and popular songs of the period like *faceta alba* ("When I met the blonde woman, my feet became lighter than Ouarzazate's stallion") that colonists and planters would belt out at cocktail time, overwhelmed by desire.

In that Eastern Europe so underprivileged today, spurned by the convoys of world tourism, ignored by our societies consumed by commerce and television, always an inch away from the breaking point, a few Traoré families and in particular Adama's, the photographer with winged shoes, had taken root like grape vines. Hair greased with lard and skin cracked by the squalls and blizzards from the great Magyar plains, their descendents settled in these mountains where the Albanian eagle and the Kosovo vulture soar together. They mixed with the natives—so much so that they dissolved into them, said malicious gossips. There are filiations through ink, love, or chance that turn out to be stronger than those of the blood, Maya.

Adama has to use a dancer's step to avoid the mood swings and puddles of ego of the models and singers he follows, and whose images he snaps for all eternity—an eternity reduced to the size of TV news and women's magazines with names like *Ebony, Me, Black* and *BB* (*Black Beauties*)[6] or *BBB* (*Berber & Black Beauties*). He knows how to coax their little pile of secrets out of them, take on their daily scratches

6. In English in the original, as is *Ebony.*—Translators' note.

and their bruised souls. To make himself indispensable, a flatterer infinitely expanding the scope of their swollen egos. In short, he's a real professional who sacrifices the expression of his personality on the altar of effectiveness. Better still, he doesn't have the swelled head of the people he associates with. Sometimes he even gives them a sharp dig coated with a thin film of humor. Who could blame him for it? He's young. He's handsome and talented. He wants to succeed at all costs ever since he left the *Museo de Arte contemporaneo* of Malabo to work behind the scenes of the jet set.

Adama is always dressed in black with a jazz musician's felt hat on his head. Physically, Adama is made of feverish, meteoric flesh. The body of an athlete, a catlike step, ironic lips. In the early hours he often has a cotton-dry mouth and the taste of Bulawayo whiskey in the back of his throat. Ice cubes clink in his brain. He rubs his eyes with the palm of his hands, his thoughts come to a halt, then take off at a gallop without warning, just like that on a sudden impulse, outside his mental space. Palpitating nostrils. Stuffy sinuses, exhausted by the night-long effort to scent out the caramel of single malts, the cherry in kirsch, the deep woody taste of flavored rums (ah, Angola rum, Maya, the weight of its bouquet!) or the twin powers of gin and vodka. He camps out, going from the Drop Dead to Crocodile Woods, drifting over to Little Jamaica and from there heading for the Bembeya Jazz Club or the Congolese Sapper, without forgetting the Baobab Orchestra, the incredibly noisy Soukouss Soukouss, and the East Abuja. Dawn finds him in the House of Nubians, with its greasy gray lounge and its stunted, lopsided zinc bar. On a Pacific blue wall, a poster of Marvin Gaye (a native of the West Coast, state of Senegal, by the way.) And under it, the lyrics of one of his songs translated into words blinding as light, sharp as glass: "Don't punish me too hard . . . Talk to me . . . Oh, what's happening? Talk to me . . . Oh, what's happening?" First-class song, first-class sound: "Talk to me, Maya . . . Oh, what's happening?" This is where he cries the eyes out of his skeleton, broken by his late-night barhopping. A charitable soul drives him back to his apartment on the seventeenth floor of Desmond-Tutu Street. He wakes up at noon. Everything is forgotten.

And the next evening, here he goes again. Back to clubhopping. The way is all marked out. Bender, bourbon, and bellowing. He won't conquer your heart like this, Maya. This is not the way he'll end his banishment, his exile in limbo. He should strike the iron of passion with a completely different stroke.

For Adama Traoré, the Other is first of all oneself. And consequently, the Other defines itself and is tested from oneself outward. One's first contact with the world, and in its wake the loved one, is through the whole body. Man remains an animal that gropes his way, sniffs or nibbles before revealing his poetic talent. It is mainly the sense of smell that is supposed to leave the most intense memory in the lover surveying the intimate geography of his lady love. As with the explorers who went out to encounter Europe, at least if the accounts handed down by our wandering historians are to be believed. Identification, recognition, the survey of European lands allegedly first went through the nose. You supposedly trust your schnozzle first, as the warthog's snout inevitably heads straight for the truffle.

Nose to nose, then skin to skin. The conqueror of yesteryear jumping from his galleon, today's tourist coming down the gangway of his plane, both feel the same epidermic vibration. The skin all at once leaving its warm African envelope for drab white innocence. The skin shriveling up, closing all its pores. The skin suddenly dried out, trembling, exhaling a strong smell. Molting, too, suddenly prone to tingling, freezing stings, cold waves at the edge of the "pallid early dawn" so dear to the poet Aimé Césaire, to snow, to the caress of wet winds, the assaults of the zephyr and blizzard, the rash-making frost, to moss and lichen, harsh winters, scattered showers, insects and swarming worms. The skin: the only receptacle by which the world is the world. Poor terrified black skin, begging to desert, swearing to skedaddle on short order. But that cannot be, Maya. Black skin is a prisoner of the whirlwind of life that takes it from ordeal to ordeal, from one deadening winter to another, from one dizzy spell to another. Then it revolts. It appropriates the blue of the sky, discovers its alabaster sisters, its white twins:

White woman, pale woman,
Oil rippled by no breath of air, calm
Oil at the sailor's flanks, at
The flanks of Jura drunks
Ibex with heavenly ties, pearls
Are stars on the dawn of your skin . . .
—MZEE MAGUILEN JOAL

And as it happens in cases like this, it (the skin, of course) dances. Dances the flamenco and the carmagnole. Swings its lard to the sound of fifes, rattles, viols, and the rhythm of the Vendean bourrée. It raises curls in the apple-green meadows. It sings the *Marseillaise* in Angoulême or Rouen in the company of rich men sporting monocles on the rue des Arquebusiers-Ivres.[7] It is swathed in sweat. It is exhilarated, it is drunk. It is a call, desire, sensuality made flesh. Now heavy with scents of milk and sperm, now with powder and fur, now with stale garlic and nettle. It gives off the odors of a shameless beast. Ordinary folks dab a drop of perfume on both sides of their nose as they pass by. No matter. With every fiber it seeks excitement, love, confusion, the disordering of the senses. It wants to merge into the skin of the Other, mix its sweat, tears, and scents with those of its like. It wants to drill into the flesh, drink the water of the Other. Follow the Other to the source, in her company. Extend its empire. Sign a neutral peace treaty with others. No domination, no negation. Emulsion, fusion. True conquistadores and not cretins of feeling. Skin against skin, bodies in harmony.

7. The Street of Drunken Crossbowmen.—Translators' note.

THREE *A Voyage to Paris, France*

In which our heroine lands in Paris and discovers a piece of French reality and its night side. The only exoticism worth anything is curiosity about the exotic. A limping angel appears to her.

My day is done, I'm leaving for Europe, you told yourself silently, with clenched jaws. You're on edge. There you are, on this evening bathed in Sahelian torpor, ready to rush into the lobby of Léopold Sedar Senghor Airport in Asmara. Your steps ring out in the halls as if in a deserted church and ricochet off the walls of the temple of concrete and glass. You are wearing a T-shirt with Nkrumah's effigy on it and Gabonese linen pants. A cap in CADU colors (Cheikh Anta Diop University of Dakar, not to be confused with the manufacturer of detergents and urinals of the same name) covers your hair pulled back behind your head and kept in place by a bow. You put on a calm face as you drag two suitcases stuffed with clothes to fight the cold, medicine against the thousands of microbes they have in Europe, not forgetting small presents for the people you'll have to deal with. You were told many times never to leave empty handed. Against your chest you carry a wallet bulging with your green passport embossed with the golden pyramid, your two credit cards, your cash and all the administrative papers necessary for this kind of trip: duly stamped vaccination card, entry and exit permits, hotel reservations with a repatriation clause . . . Forget nothing, forget nothing, be prepared for anything when embarking alone, as you are, for Absurdistan.

You arrive in Paris in the early hours. Aquarium-like silence. The only airport of the city, modest in size, looks dilapidated in the pale light of a snowy dawn. As you examine the building, you have the impression of facing a little monster cut off at the navel. The passengers had to go down the windswept railing step by step. You all ran with your head tucked into your shoulders and the French rain lacerating your faces, biting roughly into your backs. You almost grope your way into the narrow dark lobby, windy and dusty, that serves as a terminal. The baleful eyes of the customs officers are ugly from lack of sleep; they don't know what to do with their hands, which hang down the length of their body. For every passenger there are three or four of them, groggy with idleness and cheap wine—a sign that the airport is not on the verge of a nervous breakdown. You prick up your ears, their hatches wide open. You register the least detail and nothing escapes you. All around, the mood is one of lassitude and neglect as if everything were a foregone conclusion, as if the leaden weight of fatalism stopped any momentum dead. Outside, the snow is falling in a black rain.

You quickly left this uninspiring place where time moves forward drop by drop. You took an ancient taxi to the heart of the city. A shifting geography, wobbly on its rails. Barricaded neighborhoods, ghostlike outlying districts, the ultimate kingdom of snow and mud. Rust and concrete. Is this the work of a drunken architect? At the end of a long ride, you pull up to a little hotel in the Place Vendôme; all around you, wretched misery lightened by company, constantly shared. From your window on the highest floor—there are only four, actually—your eyes sweep over the gray, twisting line of the roof slates. Gloomy plain, surrounded by humid air, with the unsteady flames of a few dim lamps glimmering in it. Weary, you sink into the rough sheets, to slide slowly down into the foggy region between sleep and reverie. You finally fall asleep despite the cold and the clicking of buckets knocking together as a maid goes up and down the stairs all morning. The afternoon is a synonym of stupefaction when you go into the collective bathroom, because of the vermin and the ancient sink that splutters out muddy water. You don't touch your lunch: the doubtful bit of meat on the runny omelet does not tempt you. Quite the contrary. You give back your untouched plate to the maid with the smooth eyes of a statue.

At last you go out into broad daylight. Big flat-bottomed fishing boats made by the locals glide slowly and gloomily down the Seine, telling the ducks about their broken, crumbled-up story. At this time of day the neighborhood is swarming with activity like the depths of the Montreal souks, the cattle market of Vancouver famous for its colorful horse traders, or the zone of madams in Waikiki, that destitute rococo neighborhood just outside Honolulu. Hundreds of men coming and going, yokes of oxen pulling meat carcasses, sweating porters carrying sacks of cement and mountains of appliances labeled *Made in the United States of Africa*.[8] Everywhere you pass by the same individuals with brutal looks and black hands, crushed by exhausting labor. You can easily imagine these dog-tired peddlers beating the living daylights out of their wives. Blows against words. On the little streets with their uneven paving stones you pass the same women scurrying along, with their big bags hanging from their arms, a scarf on their heads. In the streets, you hear the same sad tune: misery, fear, and boredom raising their heads everywhere. The same kids staring at you, gripped by the vulgar attractions of a fast scam. And that beggar, a bony, awfully lanky Christ, with the lost look of shy people, who opens his mouth every time you walk past him; and you immediately notice that he has two blackish stumps in place of teeth. And those doors closing unexpectedly like sea anemones.

You have the sensation that the present goes on forever and is then replaced and slowly stitched back together. You feel like you are crossing centuries and seasons. Can this really be the country of your first mother, a country moldering at the roots, smelling of urine and need? What in heaven are you doing here? What is this place stirring up in the depths of your being? You'd have to pay me all the ore of the Transvaal to set my foot on this corner of the globe. As soon as I got there my heart would already be looking south. I would be so hungry for heat waves, roosters crowing, and siestas on shady porches. I would be starved for solar eggs, savory dishes, and lively discussions. I would have a strong desire to light up the boiler room of my body; the slightest ray of light shakes it up effortlessly, yanks it away from murky acts. So what are you doing here, Maya, for heaven's sake?

8. In English in the original.—Translators' note.

Your program can be summed up in a few words, my sweet Malaïka. Track down your first mother, the faceless woman, out of reach up to now. The one who abandoned you for reasons unknown to you. Recover her name, her face, her silhouette, at the very worst her gravestone. Spot a few tracks, a few signposts in the mist and fog, a quicksand far more unstable than the dunes of our deserts. Recover something that could sponge down your pain and justify this pilgrimage—that is your goal, isn't it, Maya? More than a pilgrimage, it's the call of the blood, the quest for origins, the beach to which the waves of your life are heading.

To accomplish this task, you have no method, no open sesame. You will trust your lucky star, as usual. You'll begin by setting up your traveler's tent for a while, melt into the landscape, learn to be accepted, while taking precautions worthy of a Masai. You know how to move among living bodies, change into the grain of sand that the ocean pushes in front of its door, get a new photo from the negative. How to roll in the ever-changing snow that hems in the meadows. To breathe in the iodized wind with open nostrils as it sweeps your hair behind your head, as it smashes up the fallen branches of the rare trees like so many stars fallen from the cage of the sky where a swarm of tiny stars is always imprisoned. To take down the tent, follow the migration of the seasons, the promise of pasturelands, the murmur of endless clouds. To avoid the sea air, the enemy of secrets, as well as the kisses of the cold.

Already the theater of your journey is set up in this corner of France. You have a solid advantage, Maya. As you very well know, you have the local color. As long as you don't open your mouth, nobody can suspect your foreign status, the source of many privileges. You usually keep quiet or else you express yourself in elementary French, as correct as possible. You try to erase your accent, which sounds like it comes from far away, as it wasn't easy to find a professor to teach you the rudiments of this language—your parents insisted you learn it, if only because of your personal history.

As soon as night has fallen, you hasten your steps to get back early. In the half-light, little blonde girls in want of customers offer up their thighs of orphaned sirens to the caresses of the wind. At the hotel, you leaf through your textbook and your bilingual dictionary, low-priced books from Ethiopic Editions, trying to get used to the new expressions produced by the language of the street.

It must be 8:00 p.m. when Titus, a distant relative of Mariette, turns up at your door. The Frenchvine must have worked miracles, you say to yourself. You recognize the young man at first sight, with his jet-black hair and his rolling gait, so faithful to the description the old women had given you. He didn't let you out of his sight all afternoon. You can imagine Titus leading a squad of the little kids who relieve tourists of their wallets and get high on the chemicals in industrial packing. You are instinctively wary of him, but the traces of an unhappy childhood on his face convince you that this ragamuffin isn't the gravedigger kind. And you lower your guard a little. And he babbles about this and that. The thundering cry of "Giddyap, go!" rises from the street. You give him another chance although you don't get the point of what he's saying right away. He tells you about music, cafés where they sell liquor strong enough to stir your blood, about natural orgiastic tableaux offered up to tourists, of places to visit. You remain on the alert, you don't let your irritation and fatigue show at all.

Slowly the conversation turns to your situation. He claims to have guessed who you are and why you've come to this place. Why you're in this state of mind, why you take various precautions. This sudden interest is finally enough to gain your confidence completely. And after all, Titus is just a scrawny cherub, limping and inoffensive. You end up telling him a bit about yourself. He paints an angelic picture of his native Normandy. You listen to him, Maya, because at heart you believe in chance and your lucky star. He listens to you in his turn, still on the doorstep, looking straight into your eyes with a concentrated air. He punctuates all your sentences with a nod of his head. You have finished, he understands that. He takes his leave very politely, bowing as he retreats. You close the door, half relieved to have spoken to someone at last after two days, half intrigued by the boy's nerve. As he goes down the stairs, he tells you he'll be there first thing next morning: he lives right next to the Place Vendôme and he knows everybody in the neighborhood.

Night. A shadowy scene. It's pouring outside. You never needed to travel to spread the wings of your imagination. Sadness covers your beautiful blue eyes. Adama crosses your mind for a moment, for you feel intermittently remorseful about him. Matters of the heart can wait, the spice of love, too. Tears of pain come into your eyes. Are you tired, or unhappy? With you, Maya, tears indicate the limit of language, the moment when words break down, shatter to bits, to debris and dust. We will remember how you have been floating between dream and reality, rejection and fidelity, yesterday and today. You are lost in the comedy of existence, that's all. Tonight you don't have the strength to face the outside world. Down and upset, you put off going outside for later. Your quest can wait, there's no rush. You've worked out your strategy as a detective: making visits, comparing contradictory archives, taking down clues, getting testimony from the rare survivors, returning to the scene of the events to untangle the threads of the enigma. The only result required is the beauty of the quest. And maybe—who knows?—unexpected and definitive closure.

You haven't come here to stock up on images and idyllic pictures reeking of kitsch: sunsets, couples dancing under the arbors, endless kisses on the squares in front of the cathedrals. No, that's not your style; with time, your works will become darker, more elusive. You remain preoccupied for a long time after Titus has left. You immerse yourself in your textbook again. You skip Lesson 1 because you find it too elementary. For you do have some basic knowledge, albeit modest and remote. After all, isn't your first mother ethnically French, very probably of Norman extraction, even if you yourself are fully African by law or destiny?

> Nabad (nabad means or connotes peace and conveys thousands of nuances): *Bon-jour.*
> Anigu waa Djamac: *Je m'ap-pel-le Jean . . .*
> Dhaktar bann ahay: *Je suis mé-de-cin/in-fir-mier*
> Waan ku daween: *Je vais te soi-gner*
> Dawo: *Mé-di-ca-ment*
> Mad bukta? *Es-tu ma-la-de?*

Caafimaad: *La santé*

Nabad gelyo (may peace accompany you): *Au re-voir*[9]

Strange, you wonder, this intrusion of medicine in a language textbook. It must be one of those works meant for our doctors, our nurses and aid workers who ease the suffering of the whole world. You can assess the vast territory of suffering in those far-off countries by such details. But you, Maya, are you really from here? You don't feel you come from here. God no, not a tiny little bit, not one iota.

You stop at the next lesson, you can see its shortcuts, its dead ends. You tell yourself that next time you'll go directly to the textbook footnotes, which are much more interesting:

LESSON TWO

Magacaa? *Com-ment t'a-ppe-lles-tu?*
Iimisa jir baatahay? *Quel âge as-tu?*
Xalkeed gashaa? *Où ha-bi-tes tu?*
Walaalo mad ledaahay? *As-tu des frè-res?*
Iska warran? *Co-mment ça va?*
Maxaad dooni? *Qu'est-ce que tu veux?*[10]

N.B. Keep in mind:

1. Our guttural *C* does not exist in French. This language wrongly spells the *K* sound with the letter *C* or even *Q,* showing a singular lack of logic.

2. The letter *X* is pronounced roughly like "eks"; it has nothing to do with our silky *X* as in *xariir.*

3. Their *H* is sometimes inhaled, sometimes exhaled. Hence inexcusable and inextricable confusions, like the pair *hiibo* and *ibo.*

4. Finally, unlike our tonal languages, with accents and clicks, French is a monotonous language, lacking in accent and genius.

That's enough for today. Is it really necessary to learn this damn language,

9. *Hel-lo, My name is John, I am a doc-tor / nurse, I am going to treat you, Med-i-cine, Are you sick, Health, Good-bye.*—Translators' note.
10. *What is your name? How old are you? Where do you live? Do you have brothers? How are you? What do you want?*—Translators' note.

mother tongue or not? A language without writing or permanent knowledge. A language deprived of glosses, analyses, manifestoes, councils, or seminars. A language without journals and of course, without an Academy or a Pantheon. No wonder the least of our nurses can set up as an ethnopsychiatrist and contact forest spirits while juggling with their totems; that the lowliest academic can pass as an expert linguist in Indo-European languages. But enough already! You'll have no problem finding a former immigrant to help you out. Titus will be happy to find an ex–garbage man from Bujumbura or an old mason who had a position in Bafoussam and still has a little stump of our international language in the back of his throat. That way you can do without your mother's dialect, the only one that managed to establish itself in this country, petrified as it is by frost and dictatorship. You are still forbidden to enter the garden of this idiom. Unintelligible words, spit out with their echo, in the crush of days and nights. Displaced accents. Swallowed syllables. The ABC of the language in a litany. You repeat for yourself.

Hooyoo: *Mè-re.*   Hooyaday: *Ma mè-re.*
Aabo: *Pè-re.*   Aabbahay: *Mon pè-re.*[11]

Hysterical laughter from the people you see, usually children who come to you in Titus's wake; you dish out leek soup to them in exchange for their smiles. Behind those smiles, their gaze never strays.

"She kept the color but she lost the language, poor thing!"

"Hey, a little more and she'll lose everything!"

A quick glance at the Ethiopic dictionary. A few verbs (ending in *id*) easy to remember, for the road. The imperative is the most useful mode, the quickest. You feel you're in a conquered country, Maya, historically and economically dominated. In the company of a people who look into somebody else's mirror to be convinced of its own existence.

Cunid: *Man-ger*   Cuun: *Mange!*
Cabbid: *Boi-re*   Caab: *Bois!*
Bixid: *Sor-tir*   Baax: *Sors!*[12]

11. *Mo-ther. My mo-ther. Fa-ther. My fa-ther.*—Translators' note.
12. *To eat, Eat! To drink, Drink! To leave, Leave!*—Translators' note.

Over and over, you keep repeating the forms of the imperative indispensable to carry on ordinary exchanges with the people here. As for the rest—that is, for your diary and your writings, the details your eye or ear has harvested—you'll set them down in the federal language, a language that covers the forty thousand kilometers of the circumference of the Earth. The universal language of diplomacy and commerce, used everywhere from Tasmania to the extreme limits of Lapland. In the same way, you'll caption your sketches and photos in the language that saw you blossom, grow like a young camel two rainy seasons old, the language that rocked the lovely tree of your childhood. You owe everything to your parents. The rest is only branding irons of your guilt, tricks your memory plays on you, the wounds of martyrdom licked out of self-indulgence: pure self-centered love.

29 *In which the heroine discovers the extent of the unhappiness of European lands and thinks about ways of finding a solution for it.*

You have decided to look more closely into this other universe haunted by the specter of belligerence. If necessary you would have come by foot, to cross visible and invisible borders, ask questions and collect answers diffracted in numerous dialects and patois, examine the scarlike traces time has left on these lands, deeply plowed by the three recent great wars. To stride through landscapes that sprung up at the dawn of the world and hunt out characters left behind at the side of the road. Set down the visions of day and the dreams of night in your imitation leather notebook. Welcome furtive things, which arrive unexpectedly like the little local trains with their trail of white smoke going up and down the basin of the lower Seine, as well as the maze of little mysterious streets on either side of the road that come together to make a village of a few hundred souls. Harvest stories in the form of moving, eternal, cruel parables. If you could, you would have imposed a *pax Africana* for the good of the local populations. Your soul and its inner flame serve as your compass.

But you, Maya, where are you really from? What woods did you come out of? Stone by stone, you build your own edifice. You've raced through your life with your elbows close to your sides without ever looking back. The result of the race: if you admit everything you owe to others, it's because you're also well aware that you didn't engender yourself, and to a certain extent you are still determined by your place of birth, your family, your culture, and your origins, since a generic, self-engendered human being does not exist. At least not yet.

Now here, it is practically impossible to escape from the proudly trumpeted *we*. The pride of being French; the pride of being from Normandy or Brittany; the pride of being Catholic; the pride of being Greek or Russian Orthodox; the pride of being Protestant. The overdoses of identity the natives consume are enough to addle their brains. Worse, they're brought up and trained to hate each other, harm each other, devour each other. Their fear of each other is exacerbated by the deep ignorance of where they are in relation to each other. An ignorance they're kept in by their laws, media, and schools copying ours. Except for a few reporters, no European you met has ever set foot on the nations across the way, for the simple reason that they've never had the right or the opportunity. And so they haven't seen what you, Maya, have seen. Even with modern means of communication, they have no way of realizing the disastrous reality of their condition. You've seen with your own eyes the houses crushed by the tanks rusting there now, the looted farms, the flattened orchards, the burnt apple trees, the decimated flocks, the roads destroyed, the five-story buildings bombed to the ground because they blocked the view of people's houses across the street. And what about the careful search of your suitcases and your person, the metal detector slowly stroking your legs, the meticulous examination of your shoes, your jacket, your bag at each checkpoint.

Here politics always takes precedence over private life: you understood it for the first time thanks to this trip to the land of France. No one has an overall view, and you can't demand that they have one. The life of the group, the clan, or the village is too important, it smothers the rest. People are naturally blinded by their own lives, their own point of view, and then by that of their group.

The constant mistake people make back home, Maya, is that they project the choices, attitudes, decisions, and policies of our federal government, our press, or our all-powerful churches onto individuals. No political analysis, as "correct" as it might be, can account for even the tiniest part of an individual's experience. This is true throughout Western Europe. But here, the gap becomes absolutely tragic. Hence aid, emergency solutions, relief. In your opinion, where do private and political life, personal history and History meet? You know the answer, Maya. You say it unhesitatingly: in art and literature. So that's where the solution lies, too: in art and literature. By Ogun, Dablé, Waaq, and Allah, it's obvious when you think of it, but the idea has to occur to you first, right? If foreign governments, including ours, really want to improve the situation in the West, they can do more and better than to play diplomatic games, multiply sterile meetings, sweet-talk dictators, and make big speeches while selling arms to them at the same time. They must act so that stories can circulate between different peoples and cities like this open-graved Paris, that sleepy Rome, or crepuscular Vienna, which could never recover from two explosions: the collapse of the Austro-Hungarian monarchy and the extermination of the Jewish elite by the Nazis. The circulation of works, ideas, and books that you hope and pray for is cruelly lacking; you wish for it with all your heart.

A bit of imagination would hurt no one and especially not the World Bank in Asmara. All you need is a handful of guineas more for aid to development to translate not only the great African, Brazilian, and European novels, but also all the great literature of the world into French, English, German, Flemish, or Italian. And you must insist that the children of Europe discover not only the Bible and the Torah, but the jewels of all civilizations, near as well as far. If narratives can bloom again, if languages, words, and stories can circulate again, if people can learn to identify with characters from beyond their borders, it will assuredly be a first step toward peace. A movement of identification, projection, and compassion—that's the solution. And it is the exact opposite of the worried—and worrying—identity so widely cultivated. Instead of the "we" so proudly trumpeted, the "we" flexing its muscles, puffing up its pectorals, it is another "we," diffracted, interactive, translated, a waiting, listening "we"—in short a dialoguing "we" will be born. And then this: you are absolutely sure, Maya, that the private, quiet dialogue of reading will really be the touchstone, the prelude of millions of dialogues spoken aloud in broad daylight. This is how peace will come into the world.

Still, I cannot be quiet for long about the discreet stirrings in my heart. I must tell you I find your logic and enthusiasm somewhat frightening. Why this hunger for otherness, Maya, this constant availability, this sensitivity so contrary to the haughty assurance of our African intellectuals who cultivate nothing but sarcasm and bitterness toward their country? You are a unique case, someone with a mental mobility unknown to our academics, stuck in the pride of their caste and the immobility of their function. But you, on the other hand, are destined for wandering, which does not mean wasting. You have a gift for fruitful nomadism; you are used to family misfortunes and feeling compassion for the misfortunes of others. That quintessence so peculiarly yours cannot be found at the center of the African empire, but on its edges, transported by people as anchorless as you are: Dunya Daher, Kossi Annan, and a few others.

What's the point of taking such pains over something that by its very essence is as short-lived as the rose? You hope to leave behind something eternal, don't you? Well then, arm yourself with wisdom and patience, for even if you painted and sculpted a work as long-lasting as the Gospels, you could also end up in the gutter like the five Caucasian workers (Jean-René Pichot, Jan Palach, Magnus Johanssson, Jesus Teixeira, and Sypros Franguiodakis: the list is running across the gigantic digital screen on Lumumba Square) whose charred remains were found yesterday under the Queen Pokou Bridge.

30 *The mystery of the two mothers is still not solved. There follows a multitude of extravagant situations that arouse noble or ignoble feelings.*

Your birth wasn't ordinary either. Your real mother, the first one, stumbled in the courtyard one day when she was pregnant with you and blind drunk. Her fall brought out all the neighbors and relatives, even your tinsmith stepfather who left his work at the other end of the town. People went on and on about your fate, they predicted that you would never be born or would come into the world badly crippled. You were catapulted out of your cocoon one month and thirteen days later. A royal silence greeted you, tongues stopped wagging, dead, glued to the palate. Your mother dripping with cold sweat, the neighbors huddled in a corner—everyone was in a state of stupor and didn't know which way to turn, overcome by a profound sensation of vertigo.

Hours later, Célestine (that's your mother's name) sat down to pick up your soft, inert flesh. She tapped you, caressed you. She massaged you from head to toe. Mad with rage and despair, she got down on all fours, turning you this way and that, weighing you in her hands with a thousand precautions. One woman in the family had a fainting spell, another tore her face, cursing, a third muttered inaudible prayers. Suddenly, the bed tipped over. Your mother slid off the sweat-drenched sheets and you with her. There you were, both of you rolling on the bed and thrown onto the dirt floor, an inch away from being burned alive by the old coal stove. Cries of panic rose to heaven. There you were, Maya, already sliding along life's course, your development hampered by the turn of events. And your first cries pierced the silence as soon as you decided to live. Crowded together in the dining room, running in from all over, people spread the word, repeating it like a mantra.

Years later, you will sprout on another soil, another continent. Cherished by another family. The little girl with her shoes encrusted with the mud of the artificial lake—that's you all right, Maya. A late-blooming child, a burst of hope for the future to her second parents. A bird-girl with an angel's name, you always pictured yourself next to many-colored birds, toucans, jackdaws, buzzards, vultures, green turacos, *talapoins*, ibises, hummingbirds, macaws, and parrots. You say "I" in order to speak better of others, you try to understand and like to explain what astonishes you. You love the spectacle of the world, including its lies, which you repeat, half dupe, half accomplice. This is why you will never stop sculpting, painting, drawing, writing (the latter more rarely, it is true, to make up for the missing part of you, unmask the blind spot of your existence.) Throwing your taste buds into the dance, driving your neurons wild. Going toward others, traveling the length and breadth of the universe because you love travel and its freight.

When someone goes to jail, you note, he has to leave the contents of his pockets at the office. Life, too, is a kind of jail officer. The officer is other people—family, friends, neighbors, all of humanity with whom you have to maintain pleasant relations. You understood all that at a very early age, at ten or almost ten, the age when one builds in one's head the roads toward the world. You felt it all again ten years later, in your mother's eyes, as she was slipping more and more into that nebulous region between life and death. A coma, that's what the medics call it. Long months without rest or respite. You and your father were at her side day and night. After she tiptoed out, you both sank into a time of darkness, a dead time in which you can't tell time by the clock.

"Never speak ill of the dead" is the ancient rule execrated by the hard of heart who resent those who have just passed over to the other side. "Death doesn't want me yet, so I'm extending my stay with these stiff-necked people, chewing away at their lives." That's so like Doctor Papa.

Never would you have wished for that blonde-haired, dirty-skinned baby to die, to disappear into the curling smoke of the past. Girl of wind and exile, never would you have wished for your first life to be told in approximations, bookish formulas like "It is said," "They say," "It seems." Can everything be forgotten? Who has the strength and the power to treat oneself to forgetfulness, like a balm to the heart? Not you, Maya. Forgetting is not your strong point, and to justify yourself you quote this Kabyl proverb: "As I was walking in the mountains, I saw a wild beast. As I came nearer, I saw it was a man. As I came still nearer, I recognized my brother."

To keep quiet would be to go back on your word, to disfigure yourself and go back on everything you stood for. But you don't have the strength to do that, either. That's why you came. Why you want to find your first mother. See the country of your first cries again. But what do you know of France, of Normandy, of those lands where prayers, tears, and poverty have centuries of existence and as many Christs on the cross in Paris, Lisieux, Dozulé, and elsewhere, too. The thirst to live their faith pushed thousands and thousands of people to walk across borders, to bring their country with them on the soles of their shoes, driven from their lands by the blows of scimitars. If you had been in the same situation as those Normans, you would have done the same thing: flee. But Providence decided otherwise for you. Your path crossed the feverish eye of Doctor Papa, who was able to arouse his wife's maternal instincts, which were pretty much in hibernation at that time. Wherever you are, whatever you do, whatever you may say, Maya, your eyes are turned to that past.

You are and you remain an exile, and what is more, exiled at the root. If you had the choice, you would say to the bones whitened under the cold marble slabs of your ancestors: "Arise and follow me to the lands of Africa, blessed by the Gods and the sun twelve months out of twelve!" It is attested that in far-off times, death was preferable to separation and deportation. It is said that many stateless people lived on foreign soil as if they were dead. Is that so certain? You doubt it. Exiled at the root, banished from the start, stripped of all your former rags, you will be welcomed in Asmara like a new penny, like a chick the first day it's hatched. You will be a young shoot ready to swallow the new rules, the new labels and the most recent hallmarks. You will be another and yourself at the same time.

In which our heroine discovers that every tragedy is first a family tragedy. The club-footed young angel guides her into the belly of Paris, swarming with mysteries.

31

You can feel it, Maya, you're getting close to your goal. You have looked for your mother for thirty-two long years. For a long time, you've been gathering information here and there. Elsewhere. Everywhere. You stock up on inner images, picked up from day to day. Gathering is your strong point. Your comfort, the compost of your emotions, the sap of your creation. Your first informant, the one who set you on the Norman trail, was indeed Mariette, the poor wretch who drags her backside and wears out her panties on our sidewalks right in the middle of the federal capital. Mariette, who holds out her begging cup in front of the Bank of Carthage, accompanied by Annette and Lucette, nicknamed "The Firefly" by Ryszard, who loves her little body from afar. Since then you have met, paid, and been in contact with many other informants who, with the exception of Titus, helped you very little; for you know nothing about your past, not even your real first name, given to you at birth by the woman who gave you life.

The nuns who took you in and kept you in an institution in Le Havre for a few weeks had left your adoptive parents next to nothing: a signed handwritten declaration (how could that poor illiterate washerwoman have written anything at all?) attesting that she would definitively give up her daughter named Marie-Anne or Marianne—the spelling is not guaranteed at this point of the investigation. Was that actually your real first name, or did the nuns invent it to facilitate your adoption by giving you a name that is almost African: Marianne is not so far from Mariam, at least to their ears.

From that time on you have stayed on the dark side of life, fertile in rumors, gossip, and other motives for guilt. Every tragedy is a family tragedy first. Only ideologues and dogmatic prophets decree that everything is political. The tyranny of the first circle, at the time of one's first steps or first spoon of soup—this is a tyranny that never disappears. It poisons your life, rips your guts out for the rest of your days, sticking in your throat like a piece of bread impossible to either swallow or spit out. In the course of these thirty-two long years, your petitions, your offerings, and your prayers will remain vain. At the end of your adolescence you may have toyed with rebellion: drugs were not far away. Religions, too. If someone got the idea of asking "But who are you?" you would answer, following the whim of the moment, "Me? A white girl, conceived in a field in Normandy, delivered by matrons, guardians of many secrets, talents, and spells, taken in by uncharitable nuns, brought up and cherished by my parents who are now growing old—a model of patience and love. Me, a white girl with straight blonde hair, an icon of our multireligious, multiracial, centuries-old federation!" Early childhood in your Norman village would later bring you the taste of hazelnut and fennel, but it's the smell of wet straw that you will be happy to remember.

"You've found me, God be praised! You're going to tell me everything. We'll know everything about your life now, won't we?" That was how Célestine greeted you. You could feel that she wanted to peel off, layer by layer, the thickness of the life you lived far from her. True, she's happy to see you again, and yet something bothers you. It is almost palpable. Could it be that a little warmth is lacking? Or is it simply cultural differences that make you think she's not very warm? She could have addressed you simply, the way ordinary people do, with words of milk and honey, using words drawn from the animal register: "Come here my little lamb, my gazelle, my kid, my sweet little camel." And yet she's as eager for you as a pig is for acorns. Something stronger than you are holds you back. You can neither advance nor retreat. You can feel your heart beating as fast as a speeding car. You have passed on your embarrassment and discomfort to her. She changes tactics in a flash. Now she's speaking the language of the heart and eyes to you, and now a boy is running up and offering to translate your exchanges.

Your knees are trembling, the tension rises another notch as she walks over to you shyly and hugs you. The adventure is over, you are filled with a serene sadness that is close to joy. You can feel her concave chest, her sickly weakness. You don't dare hug her too hard for fear of breaking one of her ribs, of hastening her death. Your face and neck are wet from the tears she has been holding back for a long time. She releases herself from your grasp, you take a step backward to look at her more carefully. You notice her dress of rough cloth. You tell yourself you could have brought her more decent clothes but you got here less than a week ago, in the middle of the night, almost at early dawn. The airport terminal was deserted, the streets of Paris poorly lit. You had such a terrible time finding the trace of this woman with her serious, gentle face—your mother now, in this little village. But you had the help of Titus, who dug again and again into the genealogical brush. A number of times you got lost in the Paris slums: with their rows of shacks without water or electricity, their low houses, potholes, dangerous back alleys, and traditional silos, they're hardly more than a series of garbage dumps. Urban decay, the architecture of resignation. It took you six hours to cover the two hundred and fifty-odd kilometers, whereas back home it would hardly have taken one hour in an underground train gliding at Mach 2 to travel the distance between Paris and this barren Normandy. Emaciated cows with bells on their necks and stocky little goats seem to have been forgotten here, with their hooves stuck in the ice. Here, man's only ambition is to remain standing, to survive. And the scrawny apple trees call for help, but it's easy to see that for them, the game is up.

"I want to wish you a hearty welcome, my child!" says your mother, and you notice her ruined teeth, the little pink veins furrowing her temples and her chaotic breathing. You examine the people, places, and things. You note that your mother, too, bears her origin like a wound and a defeat. You shiver with all your limbs, you can no longer bear this dark place, freezing like a cold storage room. You're not going to let morbid images nest inside you. You had only known this mother for a few days, the time for a handful of breast feedings, and you will probably never have the chance to catch her last words, her final tremor. Your delicate gums didn't have the time to adapt to the contours of her breasts.

Do you think you are in the world by some miracle, Maya? Where did you first see the light of day? In the semidarkness of a Norman farm, in the dilapidated clinic of a county seat, or in some gutter among the beggars? Who delivered you from your mother, who cut the umbilical cord? A tired nurse from an African NGO, or more likely a matron with skin wrinkled like a parchment, officiating right here in this land they were stripping of its trees?

You don't know if your mother was beautiful, young, and vigorous at that age. If she was a thousand miles away from this sunken, gaunt old woman with her catastrophic teeth and whistling breathing. As for your procreator, that's a different story. You're used to saying that one is not born of a father. A father is a passing thing. His absence does not weigh on you. It never prevented your lungs from filling up with oxygen and your blood from zigzagging through your veins. A father is perfectly useless, except for conception. For affection, daily life, or education, okay, but for the rest, he's perfectly useless and redundant. Your mother's circle would burst out laughing if you gave away the African customs surrounding the birth of a child with all its attendant medical precautions: weekly visits to the family doctor, bimonthly visits to the gynecologist, X-rays of the fetus month after month, and the obligatory presence of the father in the delivery room, his excitement at examining the first tufts of the baby's hair while still a prisoner in the maternal uterus, his constant encouragements to the mother, who is flapping her lips like a fish yanked out of water. The very thought of this masculine presence, this intrusion of the father into the assembly of women, would provoke the deep disgust of your mother's friends. They would conspicuously spit on the ground to show you their absolute rejection of such a custom. And you, Maya, you would pretend not to see a thing, or perhaps you would already be thinking of something else.

Days gray as a sky in Denmark, low and pallid. Sky covered with a spotless, gloomy veil, and without the trace of a human finger. Nothing like the flamboyant skies of Africa, nothing like our glowing noondays or the salt whiteness of our moon. And nothing in common either with the veritable oil slick of our African world, always on the verge of bursting into flame at the torrent of daily injustices, eternal inequalities, and televised idiocies sent out by the powerful film industry of Haile Wade. A world lost in the contemplation of its god the guinea, devoted to entertainment and consumption, entirely concerned by problems as crucial as choosing a new silent supersonic Malcolm X or a flavor of Hadji Daas ice cream or a color for the Nka living-room couch. From early childhood on, Maya, you have been committed to turning your back on that world. You always said you didn't like the kind of people who surrounded you, except for your parents.

Titus has waited up for you all night; you're almost sure of it. You size him up, you weigh him at a glance. His swollen eyes, crumpled shirt, the slight stagger in his always catlike walk. This young man did not sleep in a bed, but in all truth you don't really know. Perhaps he never had the privilege of stretching out in a real bed? Perhaps he has only known the smell of hay or the dirty swamps near the Butte Montmartre? He walks toward you with his hands in his pockets, a broad smile on his face. When he reaches you, he scratches his head like someone who doesn't know what to do with his hands. He asks if you slept well, if sleeping on it helped you make a decision, and if you were going to keep on looking. You answer "Yes." A plain, clear, irrevocable "yes."

He looks delighted. He steps in front of you, asks you to follow him. You hesitate for a moment. It's not far, he tells you. Around the corner there's a good deal, just waiting for us. You're not sure how to take the expression "good deal." It can expand or contract, depending on the latitudes. But you don't have time to waste in senseless imaginings; you're neither a tourist nor an ethnologist, still less one of those so-called travel writers who traipse all over the planet in search of utopias, heavenly oases, and stories to steal. As for them, they have already packed their bags, gone round the horizon; they're back on the road. Later, they'll break rods on the backs of sedentary people and preachers of all shapes and sizes. They have no country. They care only about words, territories, and men as they travel through these same territories.

You have entered a tiny little dark room, located in the basement of a shaky building facing the Seine. All of Paris is tightly sheathed in a coat of fog. You are expected. Two stern guards with huge mustaches and long hair, answering to the names Pilate and Juvenal, are seated behind a little low table whose only covering is a crusty layer of dirt, while a third fellow known as Père Magloire busies himself in the back of the room. You keep quiet. Your silence is your best ally, your armor. Titus walks up to the little table. With a nod, one of the three whiteys lays a big soot-colored bundle on the table. Titus gives you a few sly looks as if to say "Relax, everything's going to go fine!" You remain stony faced, you tell yourself that if you're afraid of the wolf you should never take a walk in the woods.

Suddenly everything collapses inside you. Oh, that smell, that smell! You stagger to the door. You nearly fall down three times. You drag yourself to the banks of the Seine and there you throw up violently. All around, peasants are digging coal cellars and putting up sandbags against the floods. Nobody looks at you. Once you have cleaned out your viscera, you walk up the first boulevard you encounter with a firm step and hail a cab. Before getting into the little black car with its creaky windshield wipers, you looked out for the last time, through the curtain of rain. You saw your guardian angel Titus, trotting behind you as if nothing had happened. You told the driver: "Keep going straight ahead!"

You'll have this nightmare repeatedly. The soot-colored bundle on the low table. The two scary characters with mustaches opening it in front of you with an auctioneer's precautions while the third watches for comings and goings outside, his eyes riveted on the door. And suddenly that smell. Oh, that smell of garlic and mummy! You don't have the time to move your lips to expel a word or a cry of terror. You run out to vomit.

You regained your spirits only at the hotel, when the door was barricaded behind you. You took a shower to purify yourself. Your whole body is trembling but you're sure it's only temporary. It will be over soon. You don't have the energy to bury yourself in your Ethiopic dictionaries. You decide on some light reading. You go through your bag, you come upon a woman's magazine from last week given out by the stewardess of Panafrican Airlines. You lie down on the concave bed, propping up your head on two pillows. And you go through the magazine, unable to concentrate on any of the articles, when suddenly the captioned photograph spread out on the center fold strikes your attention.

"After God gave us permission to travel safely across the world to bring light to impoverished peoples, after we built our houses and did what was necessary to provide for our well-being, established places of worship to praise our Lord, and set up a government, our next task was to increase knowledge and perpetuate it for posterity."

This profession of faith is inscribed on the marble pediment of Amadou Hampâté Ba University at Saragossa. A university for the European elite that serves as a bridgehead for African domination in the Christian West. The message does not let the shadow of a doubt remain about the spirit of conquest and mission that inspires this institution, run by superpious Puritans, very close to the Mourides of Touba, the richest in the United States of Africa.

You linger over the pictures of the campus taken from all angles. You have always been sensitive to vantage points, you talked a lot about it with Adama, in the time when you still could stand him. The time when he had the right to place a kiss on your cherry lips, the time when he was more precious to you than a collection of Baoulé weights. The campus, between the twin W. E. B. Dubois and Angela Davis libraries (both inspired by the Timbuktu model), the Moorish columns, and the purple of the tennis courts, resolutely shows the bucolic charm typical of the Horn of Africa. Kept afloat by generous donors, it attracts thousands of Caucasian, Asian, and American students. The Americans take long walks with a book in their hands, when they don't lose themselves in the solitude of a coconut grove. Every trimester it takes in one or two dissident writers, who are major purveyors of impure thoughts and choice targets for purifiers of every persuasion. Kafka, Faulkner, and Borges lived here before dying in exile.

Caucasian workers, mostly Belgians from Liège, hardly dare look at the people who are going to take the destiny of their country into their hands when they return. That's the way it goes. An idea pops into your head. Right away. That's the place you're going to send Titus, to the University of Saragossa. True, he may not have the education to pass the entrance exam, but you'll give him all the time he needs. You'll help him, and if necessary you'll use your influence with the dean. In any case, you trust him. You trust his intelligence and his resourcefulness. You're showing an ironclad optimism, an immense love for your neighbor. Through him, you would trust the whole human race. And in return, you would be doing something good for yourself, too. You would raise the pilasters of History, you would be relieved of some of the burden of your guilt.

Ah, guilt! It gnaws at your guts, my sweet little Malaïka, it sucks your blood and it would make a Zimbabwe rhinoceros lose weight. But there's no harm in doing good for oneself. Of course little Titus will get by! He was born for it: to hang onto the rudder, cling to it despite the assaults and the ups and downs, to return blow for blow and triumph over the bitchiness of life. Triumph, or slip under the water and drown forever.

At present, things are clearer. Not only will Titus get by, but he'll watch over your mother to the end of her days. He would be crazy to turn down a deal like this, an agreement completely to his advantage. You will leave him the money necessary. You will kiss your mother good-bye. You'll hug her for a long time before setting out once again. You will not linger in Paris. And you won't visit the courtyard in which Pierre Curie, one of the rare French scientists, was run over by a carriage and Marie Curie picked up the scattered fragments of his precious brain. That story had made a deep impression on you. You wanted to do a painting of it but you no longer have the strength. For the rest, it's all settled: you will follow future developments from afar. There is nothing else to be done. You will leave with a light heart.

FOUR *Return to Asmara*

32 *Our heroine returns. It is not necessary to name everything, to reveal everything.*

And now you're back, on a morning with the eternal color of dawn, daughter of the horizon. You seem at peace and reconciled with yourself. Of course you won't admit it, as usual. You couldn't live with that absence any longer, casually face the black hole that never left your side. You saw the place where you were born and set foot upon it. You will keep a vivid memory of your mother. You will help her but you will resolutely camp at a distance. For your own good and for hers, too.

Now you have found peace again. You can live again. Dream and create again. Bring comfort to the neediest Caucasians, put flowers on the grave of good old Yacuba. Only now do you feel some remorse about him. You tell yourself you should have spoken to him, drawn him out, in short lent him a helping hand. Ah! I'm beginning to know you, Maya. Your only religion is compassion and the culture of your country, which you love and hate at the same time. On this last point, I understand you completely. As an adopted child, you want to be more Catholic than the Pope in your love as well as your detestation.

Enough idle discussion. Time is short, Maya. The suitcases you're going to get back are considerably lighter. You're going to attend to the most urgent matters first. But not too much haste, either. You don't feel good: here you are already, with your sad clown face. In fact, fever is smoldering in your body. You can feel your ticker knocking against your chest over and over. You must have eaten some unwashed food, unless you forgot to take your medication, follow the directions, and the whole shebang. You'll see a doctor tomorrow, a colleague of your father from way back. Meanwhile it's hard for you to stand yourself, to say nothing of the human family. True, you did settle your first mother's situation. Just in time, you unraveled the mesh of angers that nearly destroyed you. You had a brush with death without realizing it. You were within an inch of crossing beyond ordinary limits, in quest of a fire not of this world, and found only in small quantities in drugs, in cults, or in the wake of the Devil surrounded by his idols and genies. You will no longer let yourself be overwhelmed by fatigue, by a passing feeling of distress. You will go back to your hollow reeds, brushes, notebooks, and canvases. Once again, you will lock yourself into the bathroom, close the toilet, and write. This is how you will return to your former habits, the habits of a dreamy, carefree young girl.

You will write, you will paint and sculpt under the blazing light of Africa. You'll burn yourself up in the execution of your work. Who knows, perhaps you will survive it. The journey will continue for you, Maya, in the deciphering of signs and the companionship of literature. In walking and living, too. Destiny will lead you with a firm hand toward other skies, other paths, other horizons and enchanted moons.

For the moment, you're going to visit the grave of the mother who brought you up as soon as you have caught your breath, taken a shower, and kissed Doctor Papa on his bald forehead. Before ending this meditation, you're going to tell everything to your father, who is newer to the world than an amnesiac. Everything, from beginning to end. Your faithful audience, captive and impatient, will consist of him alone. You will tell him everything in the most minute detail. You'll reel off the names of the people you met in France: first your mother, Célestine, and her family, then Titus and the little cherubs to whom you gave out soup, finally that toothless Christ and all the others, without forgetting the horrible guards who gave you a glimpse of Hell. You will describe to him the houses you visited, the streets you walked on, the taxis you rode in, the trains you took, the lands you strode through, the distances you covered, and the plans you gave up on. You will spin out the thread of the narrative to the end, and you will tell it again as often as necessary. Only in this way will you reach the first station of inner peace.

The rest will come too, but later. Much later, when your true mother will welcome you into the kingdom of her silence. When the wounds will be cauterized; when memory has finished mourning and forgetfulness has done its job. Then the world will refuse to turn into mud. You will convert the blue sky to palpable works, you will wave azure handkerchiefs in farewell.

You will also welcome Adama with open arms and heart once he has crossed his share of the distance, too. Once he has given you the flame that feeds his love and burns him up at the same time. Images, thoughts, and words will crystallize. The great poem will appear, vivid and virginal. From then on, your eyes will instantly adorn him with all the beautiful attire of passion and all the charm that befits ardor. He will have the bearing of the dromedary with its spotted robe, its head held high and big gazelle-like eyes. The dromedary? Yes, absolutely. The dromedary: icon of beauty and endurance. The male ideal, the African stallion.

There will definitely be a miracle. There will be love, and the give and take of bodies. You will go up and down the whole gamut of love, Maya. There are sometimes gleams that break through the weight of the clouds. Instants will become eternity. The clouds, a crown of darkness and rains and benediction. There will definitely be dances and more dances. And clamors of joy in the valley of life.